Just then a word seemed to ring out above the normal bus chatter. "Witch."

B listened harder. The word was probably "which" or even "wish."

"Really. A witch." There it was again. B turned around in her seat.

"A witch! A genuine, bona fide witch. Right here!" an older girl a couple of seats back said in a loud voice.

B's skin went cold and prickly. People knew! She'd only had her magic for a week, and she'd blown it already, breaking the cardinal rule that even the toddlers in witching families knew — you don't let nonwitches find out about magic.

Was it her speedy feet at the bus stop?

What else could it be?

DISCOVER ALL THE MAGIC!

Spelling B

And the Trouble with Secrets

By Lexi Connor

SCHOLASTIC INC.

New York   Toronto   London   Auckland
Sydney   Mexico City   New Delhi   Hong Kong

Special thanks to Julie Berry

ISBN-13: 978-0-545-11737-1
ISBN-10: 0-545-11737-2

12 11 10 9 8 7 6 5 4 3 2   9 10 11 12 13 14/0

Printed in the U.S.A.
First printing, October 2009

To Adam

Chapter 1

B's alarm clock went off for the third time, croaking like an angry bullfrog in her ear.

"Q-U-I-E-T," she groaned. The alarm magically stopped, and B was again grateful that she'd finally discovered how her magic worked.

B buried her head under a pillow. She'd stayed up way too late last night reading, and she wasn't ready to face the sunshine just yet. Besides, it was only 7:10.

7:10!

B sat bolt upright, upsetting Nightshade, her black cat, who'd been snoozing on B's belly. He landed on the rug and stalked away, his tail twitching.

Getting up at 7:10 was *not* good. She had only ten minutes to catch the bus and she was still in her pajamas!

She skidded into the bathroom, brushed her teeth, and combed her hair. Two minutes.

Back in her bedroom, she yanked open her drawers and tore through the piles of clothes for something to wear. Black Cats sweatshirt? Her favorite band. Always good. Purple jeans? Sure. Socks? She pulled out one pink and one green. No time to dig for mates. "M-A-T-C-H," she said. They both turned green with pink polka dots. She yanked them on.

She stuck a headband in her hair, fastened her magical charm bracelet — the one she'd received from the Magical Rhyming Society when she discovered her spelling magic — and glanced at the clock. 7:16. Six minutes down, four to go. If only she could slow down time, she might be able to eat and make the bus. But slowing down time was advanced magic, and she hadn't even had her first magic lesson yet.

If she missed the bus, no magic would avoid Mom and Dad's irritation. She threw her backpack over one shoulder and laced her sneakers.

Sneakers. Feet. She couldn't slow time, but she could speed herself up!

"F-A-S-T," she told her feet. They leaped up and sped down the stairs. Her sneakers were a sparkly blur.

Into the kitchen she zoomed, snagging the warm banana-hazelnut muffin from her mother's out-stretched hand. Her feet dragged her, knees pumping crazily, to the front door. "Bye!" she cried, her feet still churning. By the time she stuffed a bite of muffin in her mouth, B was halfway to the bus stop on the corner.

Dawn, B's fourteen-year-old sister, was waiting at the stop, her long blond hair shining in the morning sun. The bus was nowhere in sight.

Holy cats, my magic is awesome! B thought. *I can sleep in every morning from now on.*

But between one blink and the next, the bus stop was thirty yards behind her.

"Whoa!" she cried. "Slow! Stop! I mean, S-T-O-P!"

B's feet planted themselves in the ground like cement posts. But the top half of her didn't listen. She fell face-first, *ker-splat*, on the Peabodys' front lawn, within an inch of their prize chrysanthemums, smashing her muffin into smithereens.

The school bus pulled around the corner, its brakes hissing.

"Isn't that your bus coming, Beatrix?" Mrs. Peabody said, coming out onto the porch in a bathrobe and slippers. "What are you doing way over here?"

"S-sorry, Mrs. Peabody," B stammered. "I, uh, got, um, carried away! Bye!" And she raced, normal-style, to the bus stop.

Dawn stood waiting by the open doors, clearly holding the bus for B, but also glaring at her through narrowed eyes. She plucked a clump of dirt from B's hair, tossed it over her shoulder, and boarded the bus. B sighed. She knew what Dawn's look meant: *You cut it pretty close, little sis. People could have seen you. Careless stunts like that put the whole witching world at risk.*

B climbed the steps, promising herself she'd be more careful next time. It was so important that witches kept their powers secret from nonwitches. Problem was, Dawn and every other witch in the witching world made spells by composing rhyming couplets, but all B had to do was spell a word. Pretty quick and easy to do — and therefore, easy to get into trouble.

"Morning, Wonder Wasp," Jason Jameson said, his freckly face sneering at B. She shoved past him down the aisle, and plopped, out of breath, into a seat next to her friend George.

"Morning," George said, holding out a pouch of Enchanted Chocolate Caramelicious Cremes. George and chocolate were never far apart. He pushed his curly blond hair out of his eyes and did a double take. "What's with *you*? You're a mess. There's dirt on your nose."

"Is there?" B said as she tried to get it off. "I, um, tripped over my feet on the way to the bus."

She couldn't tell George what had really happened. Witches had to keep their powers secret from nonwitches, period, exclamation point. Even though George had been her best friend since preschool, she just couldn't tell him. She didn't like it, but there it was.

George wrinkled his nose. "You look like I do after soccer practice. Except, no cleats."

"Oops," B said, shrugging. "Hey, you got a new shirt!"

"Yeah, this is Sergio Vavoso's jersey," he said, pointing to his red shirt. "He's a striker for the Wilmington Warlocks, and the best striker in the world. They call him the Italian zebra, because of the white stripe in his dark hair."

"Va-Va-Vavoso," B said.

"Hey, what's black and white and red all over?"

B sighed. "A newspaper?"

"La Zebra Italiana!" He pointed to his shirt. "Get it? Red all over, like his jersey?"

B groaned. "You'll need to try harder next time."

George grinned. Then his face grew serious. He leaned out into the aisle, and looked left and right, up and down the bus, several times. Aside from Jason Jameson sticking his tongue out at a pair of girls, B couldn't see anything that should trouble George.

"What's the matter?" B asked, poking him.

"Got a secret to tell you," George said in a low voice. "Nobody else can know, got it?" He grinned. "Only you. You know all my secrets."

But you don't know all of mine. B swallowed the guilty thought. "Okay," B said. "Promise. What's up?"

"I'm starting dance lessons," George said, his cheeks turning a little pink.

"Excellent!" B cried.

"*Ssh,*" George said, looking side to side once more. "You can't tell anyone. People wouldn't get it, you know?"

B thought about it. There was nothing wrong with dancing. She caught a glimpse of Jason Jameson. No doubt, he'd tease George to death if he found out about the lessons.

"What is it that made you want to . . . y'know?" B dropped her voice.

"A lot of professional athletes study dance to improve their foot speed and coordination," George explained. "Besides, it just looks fun. The dance studio is half an hour away, and Dad and I are going on Wednesday nights, so no one needs to know, you know?"

Just then a word seemed to ring out above the normal bus chatter. "Witch."

B listened harder. The word was probably "which" or even "wish."

"Really. A witch." There it was again. B turned around in her seat.

"A witch! A genuine, bona fide witch. Right here!" an older girl a couple of seats back said in a loud voice.

B's skin went cold and prickly. People knew! She'd only had her magic for a week, and she'd blown it already, breaking the cardinal rule that even the toddlers in witching families knew — you don't let nonwitches find out about magic.

Was it her speedy feet at the bus stop?

What else could it be?

Had she given the secret away before she'd even been a true witch for a month?

And if she had, what would happen when her school, her town, her family, and most importantly, her best friend found out?

Chapter 2

"There's hip-hop, jazz, tap. The studio has ballet, too, but I'm not wearing a leotard. No way. No how."

"I'm serious. A witch. W-I-T-C-H, witch."

With each word from the girl in the back, B's panic rose. Why, why did the girl have to spell it? B shuddered.

Then she realized George was watching her, a puzzled look on his face.

Focus, B.

What had he said? Something about dancing and leotards. "Um, that's a great idea!" she said.

"Huh?"

B realized she'd goofed. "Huh, what?"

George sighed and laughed. "You spaced, didn't you?"

B made an apologetic face, then laughed, too. "Sorry."

The bus squealed to a stop. George rose, shouldered his bag, and headed down the aisle. B followed, her mind spinning. What would happen to her now? Would she lose her membership in the Magical Rhyming Society? Would she have to give back the silver charm bracelet she'd just earned for discovering her spelling magic powers? Would they — *could* they take away her magic altogether? And what about her parents — would they get into trouble, too?

B worried all the way to first period art class, and while she sketched the moon in charcoal, she racked her brain to think of a word she could spell to repair the damage she'd done. "Forget"? She could try to make the girls on the bus forget what they'd seen. But what if they forgot their mothers' birthdays, too, or even their own names? Too risky. Besides, there was no telling who else on the bus might have seen her. "Reverse"? B didn't want to be responsible for turning back time, maybe even altering the earth's rotation. Definitely not the best way to start your morning. She sighed. Magic was so complicated.

When the bell rang for second period history, B's stomach started rumbling. She thought of her mom's amazing banana-hazelnut muffin, smashed into the grass on Mrs. Peabody's front lawn, and wondered how on earth she'd make it to lunch without any breakfast. Her belly growled so loud that Jenny Springbranch, at the next desk, looked over and made a face. B decided to sneak a snack, for survival's sake.

"M-U-F-F-I-N," she whispered into her backpack, imagining a fresh muffin appearing there. And it did! When she peeked inside, there was a small, warm, crumbly muffin. A rich banana fragrance came from the bag. She reached in and broke off chunks all through class, popping them in her mouth when no one was looking.

But at the end of class, when Miss Taykin, the history teacher, asked everyone to pass up their reports, B got a shock. Her paper was gone! She had taken extra care to put a fancy report cover on it, with colored illustrations, too. And she had double-checked that she had all her homework during homeroom. How could it have disappeared?

The muffin! She must have turned her report into the muffin.

The bell rang for third period, and the class shuffled out.

"Did you turn in your paper, Beatrix?" Miss Taykin asked her as B rose, heavyhearted.

"'Fraid not," B said, shaking her head. "I accidentally ate it."

Jenny Springbranch giggled, and Miss Taykin tutted. "There's no need for silly excuses, Beatrix. If you turn it in tomorrow I'll only deduct ten points."

"Thank you, Miss Taykin." B would have to print it out again tonight.

Out in the hall B shook her fists at the ceiling. Why hadn't she thought more carefully? Thinking with your stomach was dangerous . . . and spelling with your stomach, even more so.

"No, I'm serious, she's actually a witch! She can . . ." A voice rose above the hallway chaos. A voice that sounded a lot like Jenny's. Had she seen the muffin? Heard? Smelled? Guessed?

B felt queasy. She leaned against a pair of lockers and watched kids hurrying by through unfocused eyes. She even thought about visiting the nurse to lie down. Were people looking at her funny?

B decided to skip the nurse and head for class. At least Mr. Bishop would be there. He was not only her new English teacher, he was also her secret tutor on all things witchy.

Chapter 3

Moments later, George met B at a corner in the hallway, just as Jenny Springbranch and a pack of girls passed by. Jenny made a point of looking at B, then rolling her eyes.

B scowled at their retreating backs.

"What's the matter?" George said.

"Doesn't it seem like everyone's staring at me today?" B said.

George laughed. "You're nuts. No one's staring at you. If they are, it's because you've still got grass stains on your nose. C'mon, let's go in."

B rubbed furiously at her nose. "Can't go in yet," B said. "I've got to ask Mr. Bishop something. I'll wait for him out here."

"What's up with Mr. Bishop?"

"Oh, it's nothing," B said. "Just a question I had for him about, um, something I heard." B hated to lie to George, but what choice did she have?

"Okay. See you in class." He went inside, and B blew out her breath in relief. Even the smallest things could turn into headaches when you couldn't tell someone the whole truth.

Mr. Bishop came around the corner, whistling a tune and clutching a stack of papers in one hand. His shirt and pants were dark, dark green. His clacking black cowboy boots echoed down the hallway.

She hurried to meet him halfway, out of earshot of the doorway.

"Mr. Bishop, I need to talk to you," she stage-whispered.

"Well, hello to you, too, B," he said. "I'm fine, thank you for asking."

B blushed. "Sorry. Hi, Mr. Bishop. How are you? Great. Now can I ask you something?"

Mr. Bishop sighed good-naturedly and stopped walking. "What's on your mind, B? Counting the days till your Black Cats concert?"

George had won a pair of concert tickets in Mr. Bishop's class spelling bee, and had given one to B. But that was the last thing on her mind now. She looked both ways to make sure the hall was empty, then tugged at his sleeve so he'd bend closer to her. "This morning I was in a hurry to catch the bus so I, um, used a little magic to help me get there, and I may have set a new Olympic speed record."

Mr. Bishop's eyes twinkled. "Congratulations. Nobody got hurt, I hope?"

"Only my muffin. But since then I've overheard a bunch of kids saying they saw a witch! A *real* one!" She couldn't bring herself to look him in the eye, to see the disappointment she knew would be there. "Have I given the whole secret away?"

Mr. Bishop patted B's shoulder. "Relax, B. The witching world has survived the adolescence of countless young witches before you. Your friends are talking about a so-called witch who's part of the traveling fair that's just come to town. 'Enchantress Le Fay,' as she calls herself."

Whew! It wasn't B's fault! None of those people

had been talking about her. And she'd been so sure they were.

But she was puzzled. "I thought witches weren't supposed to be public about their witchcraft?"

He let out a snort of laughter. "If she really was a descendant of the legendary Morgan Le Fay, you can bet she wouldn't be selling tickets to the fair. The real Morgan Le Fay was a powerful sorceress in ancient times. She has a garden named after her at the Magical Rhyming Society." He shuffled through the papers he was carrying and pulled out a glossy pamphlet. "See? There's Enchantress Le Fay. The traveling fair dropped off these flyers this morning, and all the teachers got one in their mailboxes."

B craned her neck to see the picture of the witch on the flyer. Great gobs of dark eye makeup, long black fingernails, bushy black hair, and a tall pointed hat. She looked nothing like any witch B had ever met. In fact, she looked a lot more like people she'd seen passing out candy on Halloween.

"So, she's a professional fake witch?" B said.

"That sounds right to me," Mr. Bishop said. "Listen, B, we don't want to be late for class. But we'll talk more about this after school, okay?"

B followed Mr. Bishop into the room. Mozart, the class hamster, waved a tiny claw at her from his cage near the windowsill. Checking to make sure no one was watching, she waved back. She and Mozart had bonded when B first discovered her powers.

"Hey look, it's Stinkbug," Jason muttered when B passed his seat. B rolled her eyes, but ignored him.

"Okay, class, we continue our grammar work with prepositions," Mr. Bishop said. The class groaned. "As you'll recall, a preposition is a little word that shows when something happened or where something is." He dropped a plastic crate of small instruments on one of the front desks. "I want everyone to take an instrument from this box, and pass it along." As the students passed the crate around the room, they took out triangles, maracas, bells, kazoos, and wooden blocks. B chose a pair of finger cymbals, and George took a plastic chili pepper filled with beans that rattled when he shook it.

"Okay, class, yesterday we learned about prepositions, so today we're going to play Preposition Percussion. I'm going to read something to you, and when you hear a preposition, let 'er rip, okay? It's an excerpt from *The Wonderful Wizard of Oz* — anyone ever read it?"

Jason Jameson snickered. "Seen the *movie* a million times."

"Ah, yes, Mr. Jameson, the movie. But before there was a movie, there was a book — a very popular one at that. You should read it."

Jason shrugged. "What's the point in reading it if I already know what happens?"

Mr. Bishop sighed. He stroked the pointy tip of his goatee. "Let's hear it for prepositions! Your objective is to make noise whenever you hear a preposition. Tonight's homework will be to circle them in a longer excerpt from the same book. Ready? Here we go."

" 'Dorothy lived in the midst —' " B clanged her cymbals " '— of the great —' " she clanged them again, and Mr. Bishop smiled over the top of his book. "That's right. 'In' and 'of' are prepositions."

He continued, "'Kansas prairies, with Uncle Henry'" — the rest of the class was beginning to catch on and starting to sound their instruments, — "'who was a farmer'" — a bunch of kids shook their instruments, but Mr. Bishop shook his head and winked at B, who had kept her cymbals silent. "'Who' is not a preposition. Common mistake." He cleared his throat and turned his gaze to the book again.

Just then the principal stuck his head into the doorway. "What is this, band practice?" Mr. Bishop hurried to the door to explain and stepped into the hallway, pulling the door closed behind him. A bunch of kids started goofing around with their instruments.

Jason was dinging his triangle like he was ringing a fire alarm. "I'm totally gonna win this preposition contest," he said.

"It's not a contest, Jameson," George said, twisting in his chair to glare at Jason. "And in case you hadn't noticed, B's been getting them all first."

"Whatever," Jason replied. "I got a magic potion from Enchantress Le Fay yesterday to make me smarter, with better-looking thrown in at no charge."

"Too bad it didn't work," George said.

"*Ooooh*," Jenny and a few of her friends said, then laughed.

"Like you know anything, Georgie-Porgie," Jason said. "Enchantress Le Fay is a real witch. And you know what? *I'm* going to be her apprentice, and when I'm a real magician, I'll make myself a rich-and-famous potion, and you'll all be sorry."

B twiddled her pencil between her fingers. She trusted Mr. Bishop when he said Enchantress Le Fay was a phony — he ought to know. But this whole conversation made her nervous.

"You serious, Jameson?" George said. "You sound like you think it's real. You're nuts if you believe in a fake witch." He started to laugh. "Everybody knows there's no such thing as *witches*."

Chapter 4

B's pencil slipped from her fingers, rolled off the desk, and clattered to the floor.

George reached down and picked it up.

B's mind was whirling. Well, what had she expected? That George would believe in witches? No, of course not. Then why did his words leave her feeling so uneasy?

George gave her a grin as he handed her the pencil. For a moment, B wished that she could go back to the good old days, before discovering her magic, when everything was normal between her and George. Could there ever be such a thing as normal between two friends when one of them was secretly a witch?

After class, George lingered by the door, waiting for B so they could walk together to their lockers before lunch. He picked up an extra copy of the homework packet and handed it to her.

"Want to go check out the fair after school? I hear they've got a decent roller coaster."

"Sure!" B said. "And we could stop and see Jason's new girlfriend, the witch." B had to see what this "witch" was all about.

George shook his head, laughing. "He's crazy. Witches and potions! That's baby stuff."

B smiled, keeping her thoughts about witches and potions to herself. Then she realized — she'd forgotten her magic lesson! Her first one was right after school. Rats!

"I can't go right after school," B said, watching George closely. "I've got, um, some tutoring with Mr. Bishop. How about four o'clock?"

"Tutoring?" George asked. "Since when does Mr. Bishop tutor? I never heard him mention kids staying after."

Oh, no. More secrets! "Well, he's, um, private about it. Doesn't want anyone to get embarrassed.

How about if I meet you at four o'clock in the park?"

George hesitated. "Okay."

After classes ended that day, B returned to Mr. Bishop's empty room. Empty, that is, except for Mozart, the hamster, who jumped off his wheel and twisted his little body around in happy circles at the sight of B.

"Hi, Mozart," B said, going over and lifting the lid off his cage. He squeaked and cheeped at her. She peeked over her shoulder, then whispered into the cage, "S-P-E-A-K!"

As if a switch had flipped, Mozart's squeaking turned into talking. "Hiya, missy, what's the matter, you got too much homework or something? How come you ain't been stopping by to chat lately, huh? I was starting to think you weren't my pal anymore."

B smiled. "Of course I am." She reached in a hand, offering it to Mozart, who climbed into her palm. She lifted him out and stroked between his soft shoulder blades with the tip of her pinky finger.

"Then I got a favor to ask you," he said. "Friend to friend. Listen, can you put a word in with the boss to get me some variety in my diet? All I ever get is box pellets, box pellets, and water. Blech. Is it so much to ask for a little celery stick now and then? A broccoli bud?" He sighed. "Some spinach?"

"The boss, eh?" B said. "Is that what you call him?"

"Yeah, and he's standing right behind you," Mozart said.

"Hi, Mr. Bishop," she said, without even turning around.

"Hi, B. C'mon, we have to go. Better turn off Mr. Talkative before he tells the janitor where we're going."

B lowered Mozart into his cage. "Bye, Mozart," she said. "S-P-E-E-C-H-L-E-S-S." Mozart silently scritch-scratched his way through the cedar chips, back to his exercise wheel.

"Ready?" Mr. Bishop asked. After B nodded, Mr. Bishop said,

"Our lesson is short, we have so little time.

Whisk us to the library of Magical Rhyme!"

"Good one, Mr. Bishop!" B said. Even though rhyming couplets weren't how her own magic worked, she was still impressed by the talented rhymers in the witching world.

Her words were swallowed up by the wind that swept through the classroom, ruffling papers on the bulletin board and setting B's hair flying. It swirled around Mr. Bishop and B like a magical cyclone, blurring the room. In a blink, B found herself standing in the great round library of the Magical Rhyming Society.

Stacks of bookshelves stretched upward for what felt like miles, and witches in glittering robes whizzed around on rolling ladders, browsing the shelves. Books and scrolls danced through the air, carried by sparkling magical spells, trailing scents of cinnamon and apples or honeysuckle.

"Before we get started, B," Mr. Bishop said, "I want to explain a few things to you. Let's sit down." He gestured toward a table. "As you know . . ."

Poof! B jumped at the magical appearance of a tall, thin woman in a sea green robe covered in silver magical charms. Her baby blue hair was twisted up into an elegant bun, and her purple spectacles sat crookedly on the tip of her pointy nose.

"Hi, Madame Mel," B said, grinning. She found it impossible not to be cheerful around Madame Mellifluous, Grande Mistress of the Magical Rhyming Society and Head Librarian of the Society's spell collection.

"Good afternoon, B, Doug," the Grande Mistress replied. "Lessons beginning, I see? Good. I'm here to give you your orientation. It's always my job. Though perhaps," she said, frowning at her crooked spectacles, "I should call it the *dis*-orientation." She straightened them. "Ready? Here we go.

"Three High Dictums of Magical Art
Which all young witches must know by heart:
One, keep your magical powers concealed,
And never to nonmagic mortals revealed.
Two, magic can't fashion things from thin air.
We move and transform what is already there,
Or conjure illusions to protect, amuse, teach.
That's the extent of our magical reach.
Three, no witch may attempt to use magic for ill,

To harm, steal, swindle, or grow rich without skill.

Those are the dictums that rule our ability.

Young witches, use caution and responsibility!"

Mr. Bishop applauded. "Excellent!" He winked at B. "She makes up a new rhyme every time."

"It was nothing," Madame Mel said, blushing all the same. She glanced at her watch, a huge time-piece with a crystal ball face and flying purple bats that told the hour. "Heavens to Pete! I must fly. I'm late for the Annual Senior Witches Rhyme Off. I'm the judge. Can't keep a room full of professional rhymers waiting. They'll have their hair in a snare or their rhymes out of time." She rested a hand on B's shoulder. "See you soon, B."

She rose from her chair and chanted,

"Don't bother with elevators, spare me the broom.

But scurry me now to the Grand Conference Room!"

And she was gone.

B blinked.

"She is a bit of a whirlwind, isn't she?" Mr. Bishop said, laughing. "Where was I?"

"Um, I don't think you'd gotten very far."

"Right. Well, then. Being a witch means you

inherit powers that most people could never dream of. But you have to make sure that you just blend in and keep your magic hidden. No one who's not a witch should ever know about our powers."

"Then how can witches be friends with non-witches," B asked, "without all the secrets getting in the way?"

Mr. Bishop's dark, sparkling eyes gazed thoughtfully at B. "You're thinking of George, aren't you?"

B nodded.

"I've seen the two of you together," Mr. Bishop said. "Remember this, B. Friendship is a magic stronger than any spell. I have faith in you. You'll figure it out."

B took a deep breath.

Mr. Bishop rose from the table. "Let's have a look around, and I'll show you some of the subjects we'll be working on over the course of your training. You get to pick what area we work on first." They started climbing one of the ladders that stretched to the top of the library. "On this floor, we have volumes and volumes on spells." They climbed to another level. "And this one has potions. These books tend to be full of strange stains, I'm sorry to say. And up here" — they reached another floor — "are charms, and above that, crystal balls. The levels beyond are advanced magic you probably won't reach until your college years." He jumped off the ladder, landing lightly, despite his cowboy boots. "Well, B, what'll it be?"

B turned to look down into the enormous room filled with books and words and knowledge. This place was amazing. So many choices, and all of them hers to devour! She turned back and looked at the spines of all the magical volumes, inlaid with silver and gold letters and glistening gemstones. She couldn't wait to read them all. But where to begin?

"Potions," she said, surprising herself with her decision. What could be more witchy than potions?

"Good choice." Mr. Bishop clapped his hands.

"Potions, from Latin 'po-tar-e,' to drink,

Will challenge my pupil to learn and to think."

The magical cyclone formed again and carried Mr. Bishop and B to a huge laboratory with shelves full of jars and bottles of colorful concoctions lining the walls. At individual workstations, witches were tossing a pinch of this and a fistful of that into shiny copper cauldrons, or frowning over tubes full of bubbling solutions. Every now and then somebody sneezed, or something popped, or someone's hair turned pink.

"Welcome to the Magical Rhymatory," Mr. Bishop said, "where new rhyming remedies are brewed up daily."

Chapter 5

They found an empty workstation. Beneath a gleaming stone countertop were rows of drawers and cupboards, and along the wall were more shelves of colorful bottles and jars.

B stroked her finger along a row of shiny bottles. "So, are potions essentially recipes? Cup of sugar and teaspoon of salt, that kind of thing?"

"Yes and no," Mr. Bishop said. "Recipes are the simplest kinds of potions. We're going to start in with the potions that really require magic."

"Sounds good," B said, still exploring the shelves. "Mr. Bishop, what is this stuff? It's not scorpion blood or salamander eyeballs or anything like that, is it?"

Her teacher laughed. "Once upon a time it was," he said. "But not now. What you're looking at is a collection of Slushy-Ice Flavored Syrups that one of my former students made last year. They give you a little energy boost, using magic instead of caffeine. She earned high honors for her mocha butterscotch." He opened a small freezer door that B hadn't noticed, scooped out a cupful of shaved ice, poured a shot of syrup over the top, and handed it to B.

"This is fantastic!" B said, chomping the ice. "It tickles." She giggled and felt a surge of energy shoot from her head to her big toe.

"She works at Enchanted Chocolates Worldwide now," Mr. Bishop said, "inventing all kinds of treats. But here's the thing: The ingredients in a potion are only a small part of what makes the potion magical. The real power comes from the spell the witch casts as she's brewing it. And powerful spells are made when the witch's mind is strongly focused on what she's doing, and how she wants it to work, and why."

B nodded.

Mr. Bishop pulled up a stool, and gestured for B to do the same. "B, how do you focus your magic in your head? How do you know what your spell will do?"

"Well," B said through a big bite of mocha-butterscotch ice, "I'm still trying to figure that out. I guess it's whatever the last thing was I was thinking of before I spelled a word. If I thought of the water in a pan and spelled 'boil,' I'd better make sure I don't start thinking about anything else, you know? It's really important not to let my mind wander."

"Exactly!" Mr. Bishop said. "Whether you make magic with rhymes or with spelled words, focus is the key."

"Then why do we even need potions?" B said. "Wouldn't spells alone be just as good? If we want someone to be happy we can just perform a spell to make them happy."

Mr. Bishop started opening cupboards and taking out equipment. "Sometimes that works," he said. "But what if you want to make the spell now, and use it later? Or give it to someone else to use at their convenience? Or ship it to Milwaukee for someone there to use?"

"Ah," B said as Mr. Bishop put a copper cauldron on the counter. "I hadn't thought of that."

"Potions are portable, *potable* magic," Mr. Bishop said. "Know what 'potable' means?"

B frowned. She hated not knowing a word.

"It means drinkable," Mr. Bishop said. "It has the same root as 'potion.'"

"*Potare*," B said, remembering his spell. "That's Latin for 'to drink,' right?"

"Bingo. Though in reality, potions can also work through the skin, or by breathing in their vapors, though not always as well." He gestured toward the cauldron. "Let's get started. I want you to try to make a simple laughing potion. These drawers and cupboards are full of ingredients — the fridge, too. Help yourself to anything you see."

B wasn't sure where to start. "I can just pick any-thing?" B asked. "Isn't there a book I can look at?"

Mr. Bishop shook his head. "Just trust your instincts."

B tossed her slushy cup in the trash and rubbed her hands together. This could be fun. Looking through the drawers and cupboards, B found rubber bands, matchbox cars, playing cards, bits of fabric and string, rusty nails, twigs, old pennies, marbles, some colored hair bands, old stickers, clothespins, beads, and odds and ends she couldn't even name.

"I thought the ingredients would be, um, spices and things," B said. "Herbs. Oils. Stuff like that. This drawer is full of junk." Row after row of drawers revealed the same assortment.

B opened the fridge. "There's nothing here but Swiss cheese, mustard, and pickles!"

"I was sure there was bread in the cupboard," Mr. Bishop said, nosing around. "Nothing helps a potion like a cheese and pickle sandwich. Do you like mustard?" He found a bag of bread and set it on the counter.

B was baffled. "Am I supposed to put a sandwich into my potion?"

"Certainly not," he said, pulling two slices of bread from the bag. "You *eat* the sandwich. Gets your creative juices flowing." He started spreading the mustard. "C'mon, B, think. A witch rarely has powdered diamonds and dried rosemary when she needs them. But everyone's got a junk drawer. Part of witchcraft is learning how to make do with what you've got. So, find some ingredients that you think suggest laughter, and brew them up."

It sounded mumbly-jumbled to B, but who was she to argue? She poked through the drawers and cupboards. She selected a joker card, a frog-shaped pencil eraser, a bubble wand, and a fake feather.

"Feather?" Mr. Bishop asked through a mouthful of sandwich.

"For tickling," B said. "That always makes me laugh. Oh, wait, one more thing." She reached into the jar with a fork and pulled out a pickle.

"Pickles are funny, don't you think?" B said. "Just saying the word makes me smile."

"I never thought of it that way," Mr. Bishop said. "Usually pickles make me hungry."

B tossed all her ingredients into the cauldron and stared at them. They sat on the shiny bottom of the pan, doing absolutely nothing, looking like bits of clutter, not like the pieces to a magical puzzle.

"Well," her teacher said, "at this point in the process I would usually instruct my students to think up a *rhyming* spell to bind the potion together and create the liquid. So, let's see what you can do with word-spelling."

As she munched on her sandwich, B wondered what word she should spell. She decided she'd try the obvious one. She tried to focus on the sound of laughter, but it was hard to ignore all her stray thoughts.

"L-A-U-G-H-T-E-R," she spelled, but a bit of sandwich almost caught in her throat. She hoped it wouldn't mess up her potion. Soon, a bubbling sound came from the cauldron. She peered in to see the ingredients melting away like ice cubes, forming a pool of amber-colored liquid. When it was done brewing, Mr. Bishop poured some into a cup, took a deep breath, and drank. A little puff of cloudy vapor rose from the mouth of his cup, then vanished.

"Hm," he said. "*Hic!* I'm not *hic!* laughing. *Hic!* I seem to be *hic!* — uping."

"Oops," B said.

She waited, embarrassed, for the hiccuping to stop. At last it died down.

"Fortunately, I didn't drink much." Mr. Bishop wiped his mouth on his sleeve and he said:

Recycle the magic, rekindle the spell.

Polish the pot and perform the charm well."

B's cauldron emptied as little whirring objects leaped out of the cauldron and hopped back into an open drawer. B could barely see what they were, except she knew they were unfamiliar. "Hey, those weren't the things I put in," she said. "What happened?"

"I drank some of it," Mr. Bishop said, "which changed the individual components. Now, try it again. You had the right idea with your ingredients but I think you lacked a little focus."

B tried again, this time with other ingredients: a tiny plastic rabbit, a ripe strawberry, a bit of paper folded into an origami swan, a quarter minted the year she was born, which, naturally, made it lucky.

She spelled "laughter" again and tried to concentrate. Mr. Bishop took a sip.

"Iiiiiii'm not feeling funny," Mr. Bishop warbled in a lovely bass singing voice. *"Iiiiii just feel like singing! Sing, sing, sing, sing, singing my cares awaaaaaaayyyy . . ."*

All the other witches in the laboratory turned to watch. B desperately wanted to duck down below the counters and wait till the tiny smidge of potion Mr. Bishop drank wore off.

At last Mr. Bishop's mouth clamped shut. He loosened his collar, blushing even brighter than B. "Whew!" he said. "That was a first."

"You could teach music," B said, "but maybe I should test my own potions. C-L-E-A-N," she told the cauldron, then to her teacher she added, "It would save you the risk."

"As your teacher, I need to test them to see if they work, or I won't know how to help you fix them," Mr. Bishop said. "But listen, B, this is important. Don't make any potions at home and give them to anyone. Not until I've signed off on them, okay?"

"Sure," B said. She couldn't imagine a reason why she would. "My potions wouldn't even polish the furniture."

"Nonsense," her teacher said. "You're off to a great start. Your potions are doing *something* — just not the something you want, yet. Be patient. Some witches just plain can't do potions at all, did you know that? Now, let's have one more try with the laughter potion. Maybe change the word you spell a bit. "

B sighed and searched yet again for ingredients. She found an empty soda can, which reminded her of a hilarious moment in a movie. She found a bit of cord, which made her think of microphones and stand-up comedians. And she found a dog collar, which reminded her of George's dog, Butterbrains, who was always "playing dead," sticking his long shaggy legs up in the air. "L-A-U-G-H," she spelled, half giggling as she said it.

Mr. Bishop took a taste, and immediately started chuckling. "You've got it! Ha-ha!"

"I think I get it," B said. "Or I'm beginning to. It's not enough just to think about laughter. I have to really get myself in the right frame of mind. So in this case, I had to get myself laughing!"

"You're on the right track. Hee-hee! Pour the rest into a bottle, and stopper it. A good laughing potion is always valuable." B did as her teacher said. "This potion earns the Bishop Seal of Approval. Congratulations on an excellent first lesson. Now, let's go back to school."

Chapter 6

As soon as Mr. Bishop deposited B back in the English classroom, she sprinted out of the school and down the street toward the park. Her watch told her she only had five minutes to reach George at the park. *Speedy feet sure would come in handy now*, B thought. But she knew better than to try it. She used her Crystal Ballphone — a recent gift from her parents in honor of her finding her magic — to make a quick call home, letting Mom know about her plans to go to the fair, and her first-ever potion at her first-ever magic lesson. Mom was proud, as B knew she would be.

All in all, she was only three minutes late when she found her friend alone on the swing set, swinging so high it looked like he'd flip over the top. Behind him, flags and banners from the huge white grandstand tent of Merlin's Spectacular Fair flapped in the breeze. George scuffed his feet in the dirt to slow down.

From behind them, calliope music blared. George and B turned just as a unicyclist burst out from the entryway. A juggler and a fire-eater stood on either side of the colorful arch, demonstrating their skills, and a hawker shouted a welcome at passersby.

George and B looked at each other. "What are we waiting for?" George asked. "Roller coaster, here we come!"

They bought their entrance tickets and hurried through the turnstile.

"Cotton candy!" George ran to a vendor and came back with a big blue blossom of spun sugar. "Want some?"

"No, thanks," B said. "I want a candy apple. Then I want to find Enchantress Le Fay!"

"Huh?" George seemed to be having trouble unsticking his bottom jaw from his top because of the cotton candy. "Whynf . . . oomp . . ." He swallowed. "Why d'you want to see her?"

B hated that she couldn't explain the real reason for her curiosity. She dodged the question with a question. "Aren't you curious about her, and those, um, crazy potions of hers and stuff?"

"Nah. I want to see the trapeze artists. And hit the rides."

B glanced at a big poster that showed the schedule of all the fair shows. "The trapeze show doesn't start for half an hour. And the rides will be more fun when it gets darker. Don't you want to see what Jason's so excited about?"

George tossed his stick in the garbage. "Okay," he said. "But then it's go-cart time!"

"Deal." They set off to look for Enchantress Le Fay.

"Step right up, step right up, ladies and gentlemen, for a sight you won't see every day!" A barrel-chested man with a red tuxedo and a black handlebar mustache stood outside a large booth surrounded by black and purple drapes, shouting in a megaphone. "From the far reaches of time, from the dark forests of Olde England, comes a living descendant of Morgan Le Fay, the sorceress who bedazzled King Arthur's court! Need a love potion? A cure for baldness? Searching for the elixir of life? Look no further! Enchantress Le Fay waits to help you!"

Several people passing by stopped, and soon a good crowd was gathered.

Then, the mustache man pulled a rope, which separated the two halves of a frayed and faded curtain, patched in parts. Plumes of gassy green vapor billowed forth, making B's nose itch. When the mist cleared, the first thing she saw was . . .

"Jason Jameson!" George wrinkled his nose.

Sure enough, standing next to the enormous cauldron, with a huge smug smile on his freckly face, was their classmate from English.

Jason caught sight of George and B in the audience and made a big show of pinching his nose like they were skunks. He only stopped when Enchantress Le Fay made her grand entrance onto the little stage.

She was tall, with thick, frizzy black hair streaked with white at the temples. But she didn't look old. Her skin was smooth, and plastered with makeup. She wore a tight black dress that buttoned in front with hundreds of tiny black buttons, but hung in torn strips around her knees, showing her tall, black pointy-toed boots. Around her neck were dozens of chains bearing heavy brass charms, or leather pouches of something or other. The tip of her witch's hat bent downward in the back, but Enchantress Le Fay stood stiff and straight, her eyes closed, her chin thrust high in the air as though she were sniffing the wind like a hunting hound.

"Gather 'round, gather 'round, ladies and gents," Jason called out in a failed imitation of the mustache man. "I, Jason the Magical Prodigy Apprentice, announce . . ." Enchantress Le Fay elbowed him, scowling. Jason gulped. "Er, the show's about to begin."

The crowd surged forward, sweeping B and George along with it.

They waited.

Enchantress Le Fay breathed.

And then she screeched. "I . . . SENSE . . . SUFFERING!"

Everyone jumped. She had a gravelly kind of voice, sort of like Dawn's sounded the morning after a softball tournament, when she'd been cheering for twelve hours straight.

Now the so-called witch's eyes were open wide — wild and frantic. She jerked her head this way and that, pointing randomly to different people in the audience.

"You!" she said at last, pointing to a heavyset man in the back of the audience. "Do you *still* grieve at the death of a parent?"

The big man's jowls quivered. "H-how," he sniffed, then burst into loud sobs. "How did you know about M-Mother?"

People in the audience gasped. Enchantress Le Fay took a small bow. She pulled a little bottle from the sleeve of her dress. "Apprentice," she ordered Jason, "take this to our suffering friend. For fifteen dollars, my sadness remedy will heal his broken heart."

The man counted out the bills, downed the contents of the bottle, and left beaming and blowing kisses of gratitude to Enchantress Le Fay.

"For crying out loud," George said to B. "What a phony! I saw that guy counting change in the ticket booth a few minutes ago."

B stifled a laugh. Enchantress Le Fay shot an angry glance at George, then cleared her throat. "Apprentice," she said, "fetch me my case!"

Jason disappeared behind the curtain, then returned dragging a large, dingy suitcase. He pulled a lever, and telescoping legs popped out from each corner. After some fumbling with the latch, he opened the case, revealing a traveling pharmacy full of vials of liquid, all in tiny corked green bottles.

Enchantress Le Fay gestured across the surface of the suitcase with a sweeping motion, trailing the loose fabric of her sleeves. "My friends," she cried, "how much *need* I sense among you! Painful joints and lonely hearts! Aching teeth and boring jobs! Naughty children and bad grades! Oh, *oh*, the suffering!" She pulled a red silk handkerchief from the bosom of her dress, and dabbed at her eyes. "Here in my stores you'll find the fruits of a *lifetime* of study and toil! And I offer it all to you, starting at only five dollars a bottle. But that's not all! At Friday's Grand Spectacular Show, on the last day of the fair, I shall demonstrate cures and remedies so astonishing, they'll curl the hair on your toes. Come one, come all! Bring your ailing aunts and uncles! But don't wait until Friday. Step up now to relieve *your* suffering."

Enchantress Le Fay gave Jason a sharp nod. He looked confused for a moment, then began calling, "Step right up! That's it, step right up, ladies and gentlemen, form a line, don't all try to be the first to sample Enchantress Le Fay's magical cures!"

B shook her head in disbelief. *This* was what people thought of as a witch? This ... this tacky show-off? She tried to picture her mother, who was both an excellent cook and potions mistress, dressing up in those phony rags and strutting around like Enchantress Le Fay. The idea was preposterous.

"What's funny?" George said, nudging B.

"Oh, nothing," B said. "Want to get in line and have a peek at the potions?"

George grunted. "No point. I can't believe all these other people are lining up. There's *no such thing* as witches!"

A little hush fell over the people lined up in front of the cauldron. It seemed as if everyone looked first at George, then at Enchantress Le Fay, to see what she would do.

She scanned the crowd, then thrust both hands out wide so that her long, spooky sleeves flapped like bat wings. "There are always those who doubt or deny my power," she said in her screechy voice. "Young man, I was peering into the secrets of eternity before you wore your first diaper."

George shrugged. "Maybe you should have worn glasses."

All the eyes moved back to George. It was as if a tennis match had sprung up between B's best friend and the wannabe witch.

Enchantress Le Fay pointed a long-nailed finger at George. B couldn't help noticing that the witch's nails were painted green, with black bats on each nail.

"I am not in a mood to be vexed by unbelievers," Enchantress Le Fay said. "You don't believe witches exist?" She cackled with TV-witchy laughter. "I'll prove it to you."

Chapter 7

Enchantress Le Fay whipped her hat off her head, and held it up for all the audience to see that it was empty. She pulled a wand out of her sleeve and tapped the upturned brim of the hat. *"Hoobedy doobedy fizzledy-hop!"* she cried, then pulled a white rabbit out of her hat.

There were *ooh*s and *aah*s from the crowd as Enchantress Le Fay held up the squirming bunny for all to see, but George wasn't impressed. "Any magician could do that with a trick hat," he said. "Easy peasy."

"Hmph," Enchantress Le Fay snorted. She handed the rabbit to Jason and shooed him away. With a long paddle, she stirred whatever was in her great black cauldron. Wafts of vapor emerged, which she waved through the air with strange hand motions. "Tell me, Cauldron," she cried, "is there anyone here, besides me, who possesses a witch's skill and talent? Boil once for yes, and twice for no!"

Her cauldron bubbled up, releasing more jets of vapor, not once, but twice.

"I thought not," Enchantress Le Fay said smugly.

A lot you know, B thought, but she kept her mouth shut.

"There's probably a button she's stepping on," George said. "C'mon, B, let's go ride the rides."

But Enchantress Le Fay wasn't done with George yet. "You," the fake witch said. "Boy with Glasses. You're not *afraid* of my powers, are you?"

George pushed his glasses up the bridge of his nose. "As if! You're about as scary as a stomachache."

The would-be witch pulled two large bottles from a table behind her. She poured amber liquid from the first bottle into an old-fashioned goblet, muttering "dragon's tears...." She shook some powder from a pouch around her neck and swirled it into the cup. "Serpent's teeth . . ." Then she uncorked the second bottle, and with trembling fingers, prepared to pour some of it into the cup. "Morning dew." She closed her eyes. "Oh, should I do it? Is it too cruel? No! He needs to be taught a lesson!" Her eyes flew open. "Stand back, everyone!" she cried. "This potion" — she glared at George — "*curses* the unbelievers who deny my power. Beware!"

George laughed aloud.

Enchantress Le Fay poured the other bottle into the cup. It bubbled and frothed instantly, pouring over the mouth of the cup in foaming blobs.

"Just as I feared," she hissed. She pointed a green-tipped finger at George. "This curse will remain in force upon you, until the day you crawl back to me, declaring my powers are real and begging me to reveal my secrets to you!"

She threw the contents of the foaming goblet into her cauldron. There was another burst of stifling green smoke.

A handful of people clapped. The smoke cleared, and Enchantress Le Fay's triumphant face appeared.

What a phony, B thought. *A mean, annoying phony.*

But George only laughed. "Vinegar, detergent powder, and soda water," he said. "Anybody can do that trick."

"C'mon, George," B said. "I've seen enough. Let's get out of here."

"Yeah," George said, following B toward the rides. "I'll bet you've seen enough this afternoon to know for sure that witches aren't real, right?"

Um . . . B forced a laugh. George would never know just how much proof she had that witches *were* real! Time to move the conversation to safer ground. "Look!" she said, hurrying away from the tent. "There's not much of a line by the go-carts."

They paid for their tickets and went roaring around the track, kicking up clouds of dust thicker than Enchantress Le Fay's smoke screens. But when George's go-cart was halfway around the track, it stopped, and B bumped into him. George tried and tried to restart the car, but it didn't respond. Cars piled up behind them, and people hollered out to see what was wrong.

A fair worker with "Snowball" tattooed in big letters on one arm came over to investigate. He ordered George to climb out of the cart and then moved it off the track. He pulled B's car off, too, as she joined George.

"Well, look who's here," a voice said. "Bee Sting and her sidekick, Georgie-Porgie."

It was Jason Jameson, leaning over the fence to jeer at them, a candy straw dangling between his teeth.

George ignored Jason. But when a group of teenagers who'd been stuck in the traffic jam zoomed by and yelled, "Hey, little kid! Learn to drive!" and Jason started laughing, B could see George's patience start unraveling.

"I *know* how to drive it," George said, kicking a tuft of grass. "The stupid car stalled."

"That's 'cause you're cursed," Jason said. "Enchantress Le Fay got you good."

"Don't you have a plastic cauldron to scrub, *apprentice*?" B said.

"Yeah," George said. "Go refill her bottles of vinegar and soda. Potion, my eye. That's the oldest chemistry trick in the book."

"So what if it is?" Jason said. "When a real witch does it, it still makes a curse. And you're the one that's cursed."

Chapter 8

The next day, George wasn't on the bus. B watched for him all morning, but when she arrived in Mr. Bishop's room for English class, there was still no sign of George. B fed Mozart a baggie full of celery sticks, and laughed as the hamster snarfed them like a kid eating Halloween candy. But all the while she wondered, where could her friend be?

Mr. Bishop started reviewing last night's homework, and a few minutes later, George burst in. His "La Zebra Italiana" jersey was inside out, and his hair, which was always a bit of a shaggy blond mop, was practically standing upright. He ran into the room just as Mr. Bishop was collecting the preposition packets.

"Mr. Bishop, can I call my mom? I can't find my homework, I think I must have left it at home. My mom might be able to drop it off for me."

"No need to interrupt your mother's day over this," Mr. Bishop said. "Stop by my desk after class and we'll figure out what to do about your assignment, okay?"

George sat next to B. His face was drawn, his lips pressed tight together.

"*Cursed . . .*" Jason hissed, just low enough for Mr. Bishop not to hear.

Later, when Mr. Bishop stepped out into the hall for a second, B whispered, "George, what's up?"

He shook his head. "I can't say."

B gave him a friendly jab with her elbow. "You're not keeping secrets, are you?"

George sighed. "Later, okay?"

On their way to lunch, when Jason was nowhere near, B asked George again what was wrong. He looked away, but B teased him for an answer. Finally he relented.

"I overslept this morning and missed the bus," he said. "Burned my toast. Broke a glass. Banged my head on a cupboard door, and my mom got a flat tire driving me to school. And, I forgot my homework."

"I'm sorry," B said, squeezing his shoulder. "What a rotten start to your day!"

"It's that curse," he whispered. "I didn't think so last night, all that mumbo-jumbo and the vinegar trick. But after this morning, I don't know. Maybe it is real!"

"But that's ridiculous, and you know it!" B burst out. "One: You're always running late in the morning. So that proves nothing. Two: Anyone can have a bad day. Three: Enchantress Le Fay is not a witch. *That's* obvious!"

They reached the lunch line. B glanced at the board where the entrée was displayed. Oh, no. Shepherd's pie. A fancy way to say dried-out potatoes over gray meat glop, with the occasional pea that was even grayer than that meat. George hated shepherd's pie day, and B worried that he'd see it as more proof he was cursed.

B put a hand over her mouth. "L-A-S-A-G-N-A," she coughed. A tray of carrots turned into a hot pan with melting mozzarella slathered over ruffly noodles and bubbling sauce.

"Look, George," she said, trying to sound surprised. "One of your favorites!" Without waiting for his response, B told Mrs. Gillet, the server, "We'll both have the lasagna, please."

Mrs. Gillet scratched her chin, frowning at the hot pans. "Marge," she called to the back kitchen, "how'd you have time to make a lasagna this morning without me knowing?"

"They don't have any garlic bread," George commented. B bent over, pretending to tie a shoe, and spelled "garlic bread," thinking hard about the breadbasket.

"Are you sure?" she said, popping up. "Check again."

"I've gotta get me some more sleep," Mrs. Gillet mumbled, loading up their plates and looking as if she'd seen a garlic bread ghost.

"That's lucky, isn't it?" B said on their way to find seats. "Lasagna on today's menu?"

"I guess." They found a table and sat down.

B dived into her food, hoping George would follow her lead, but he barely nibbled his lunch. Soon B's garlic bread felt like stale crackers in her mouth. She hated to see George so down, and for such a stupid reason, too. What good was magic if it couldn't even cheer up a friend? She thought of Mr. Bishop's reminder that friendship was a magic stronger than any spell. Maybe what George needed more than potions and "luck" was a best friend who cared.

"You haven't told me any corny jokes all day," B said. She reached over and felt his forehead. "I think maybe you need to see the nurse."

George perked up a little. "What's black and white and green and black and white?" he said.

B grinned. *That* was more like it. "I dunno, what?"

"Two zebras fighting over a pickle."

"Aw, man!" She crumpled her napkin and threw it at him. "That wins a new prize for cheesiest joke ever."

A smile was doing battle with George's face, and

winning. He took a big bite, then another, and said, "I got another one."

B gulped a mouthful of lasagna. "Let's have it."

"What's green and black and white and green?"

"Um, what?"

"Two pickles fighting over a zebra!"

"I was wrong," B said. "*That's* the cheesiest joke ever." Her old pal was back! She'd broken the so-called curse.

George wiped up the last of the lasagna with his garlic bread, then stood to leave. "C'mon, let's get to gym early and play Horse," he said. But on his way to dump his trash, he tripped on a shoelace. His untouched cup of butterscotch pudding went flying . . . and landed, *plop*, all down the front of his jersey.

Every kid in the cafeteria burst out laughing.

B picked up the things that had fallen from George's tray and helped him dump his stuff. Then they hurried out of the cafeteria.

"I'm doomed, B," George said, looking shaky. "What if the rest of my life is like this? I'll be like the cartoon character who has a piano drop on his head every day!"

"Don't be silly!" But B wondered . . . could it possibly be true?

Later in science class, George and Jason were randomly assigned to be lab partners for a project involving a Bunsen burner. "I don't want to work with *him*," Jason said, hamming it up for the whole class. "He's cursed! I'll end up burned like crispy bacon!"

B knew she shouldn't take magical revenge on Jason, but she got through her anger by thinking of the words she'd use if she did. "Chicken pox" was high on her list, as were "blistering warts" and "soaking wet."

Mr. Lorry, the science teacher, who most days seemed half deaf, didn't even try to stop Jason from bragging, "I'm going to have Enchantress Le Fay make me a curse-repellent potion to ward off any contagious evil sticking to this guy."

Jenny Springbranch tittered.

When the dismissal bell rang, George and B headed for the bus.

B had to do something to cheer him up. "Want to go to the fair again?" B asked. "We never did try the roller coaster."

"No, thanks," George said. "I don't want to be anywhere near Enchantress Le Fay."

"Oh, come on," B began, but she stopped when she saw George's stricken face. Now wasn't the time to tease him.

A clap of thunder struck, and in a matter of seconds, from seemingly nowhere, a rainstorm rushed in, drenching them. B shielded her head with her bag while George fumbled in his backpack for a travel umbrella. The sidewalk danced with raindrops as sheets of wind-blown rain slashed across the parking lot.

"Hurry!" B called. "I can't believe this storm."

When George finally popped his umbrella open, gusting winds took hold of it and flipped it inside out.

"Holy cats!" B cried.

"Unbelievable," George said, looking at the umbrella corpse.

"Where's the bus?" B said, shielding her

face with her backpack. "We're gonna get soaked!"

"We're already . . ."

"Watch out!" B cried, leaping backward as a car drove by, close to the curb. A huge puddle had formed in the flash-flood conditions, and B and the others in line for the bus managed to jump back in time.

But not George.

A sheet of muddy water plastered him as the car sped past.

"You see what I mean?" George said, looking despondently at his shirt, which was now the color of butterscotch pudding. "Plain and simple: I'm cursed."

Chapter 9

After dinner and homework time that night, B showered early and got into her pajamas. She crawled under the covers, and Nightshade, recognizing his usual invitation, jumped up and started kneading her belly with his paws.

"Geez, cat," she told him, scratching between his ears, "I'm not a pillow."

After reading for a while, she turned off the light and lay in the dark, worrying about George. Finally she picked up the phone.

"George isn't feeling well, B," his mother told her. "Let me check to see if he can take your call."

When he came on the line, George's voice

sounded thin and raspy, like he was 110 instead of 11 years old. "H-hullo?"

"What's the matter with *you*?" B asked. "You sound terrible!"

"I'm sick." He wheezed. "It's getting worse. The witch's curse did me in."

"Oh, for the love of chocolate," B said. "Stop being so melodramatic! One teensy little cold, and you're getting hysterical!"

George didn't say anything. He only coughed.

B fumed. Here she was, calling to be a comforting friend, but that stupid curse kept getting in the way.

"Well, I'll see you tomorrow, anyway," she said.

"Doubt it," George said. "I'll probably be under quarantine."

B gave up. "If you say so," she snapped. "G'night."

"It's been nice knowing you, B," George said gloomily. "You can have my lucky soccer ball. You know. Just in case."

"Good night, George."

" 'Night."

B hung up the phone, then thumped her mattress with her fists. "Aaaargh!" Nightshade stalked away in disgust, the tip of his tail refusing to curl.

B lay in her bed for a long time, thinking. This had to stop. She wasn't about to let magic, real or fake, come between her and her closest, best, most loyal friend. And the first order of business was to get rid of Enchantress Le Fay's fake curse. The only question was how.

Sure enough, the next day George was absent from school. B spent the morning debating with herself what to do about him. By the end of English class, she'd made up her mind. She hung back after class to corner Mr. Bishop.

"What's on your mind, B?" he asked after the room had cleared.

"It's George," she said. "I need your help." B explained about Enchantress Le Fay casting a bogus curse on George at the fair, and about how George had been on a downward spiral ever since. "I've tried to use magic — and just plain old friendship — to cheer him up, but so far nothing's worked."

Mr. Bishop straightened his eggplant-colored sweater. "What would you like me to do about it, B?"

B wasn't sure she had an answer. He was a witch, wasn't he? An expert? He should know what to do.

"Well," B said, "I've been wondering. You said that witches couldn't be public about their powers without breaking all the rules. Right?"

Her magic tutor nodded.

"Could it be possible that Enchantress Le Fay is a real witch after all, hiding behind the costume of a fake one? Because as soon as she cursed him, bad things really did start happening."

Mr. Bishop stood up and stretched, like a cat waking from its nap. "B, I really don't think that's likely."

"But it's not impossible, is it?" she said. "You'd be able to tell if you met her, wouldn't you? Or if you tested one of her potions?"

Mr. Bishop sighed. He took off his glasses and nodded.

"Then, will you come with me after school today, and prove once and for all if she's a real witch?"

Mr. Bishop twirled the curl of his pointy goatee around his finger. "I suppose . . ." he mused. "This could be a useful part of your magical education. We'll meet at the fair just after school."

Right after the last bell, B rushed to the fair and was surprised to find things quiet. It looked desolate, with soda cups and French fry trays cluttering the ground, and all the game stalls empty or with only one customer. There was no sign of Mr. Bishop, and B guessed she must have gotten there before the afternoon rush. She decided to look around while she waited. Maybe she could find out some things for herself about Enchantress Le Fay.

Behind the fairground stood a row of Dumpsters, and beyond that, a dozen or so trailers and campers were parked. That, B figured, was where the traveling fair workers lived. She walked along, reading the crazy bumper stickers from the Grand Canyon, the Everglades, Niagara Falls. What a life it must be, traveling the country with a caravan of colorful characters!

Then B saw a small trailer painted with black and green stripes and a license plate that read RCH WTCH. *Rich witch? That must be Le Fay.*

A flickering light shone from one of the windows. Was the light a sign of something magical? She had to get a better look.

B tiptoed closer and could hear Le Fay muttering to herself. What was she up to in there? More potion making? B peeped through a gap in the curtains. The light flashed again and B saw that it was a television playing an infomercial for some magic makeover cosmetics.

Enchantress Le Fay was flitting around the trailer, trying on rings and bracelets. Only it looked nothing like her. Her hair was short and blond. She wore a long, faded T-shirt and a red bandana in her hair. Every now and then she took a bite from a jelly doughnut. She wasn't brewing up potions after all.

Maybe Le Fay wasn't a witch. B decided there was one more place she could look for clues, especially while "the witch" was off duty.

She rushed back to the little tent, hoping to get a good look before Enchantress Le Fay came out for the afternoon show — and before Mr. Bishop showed up. It was busier now, but the area around the Enchantress's stage was clear. B looked around, saw that no one was paying any attention, climbed the steps to the stage, and parted the curtain.

There stood the huge cauldron, looking a lot less impressive up close. It stood on a black rug. B lifted one corner of the rug and saw electrical cords running from the cauldron's bottom to a power strip at the rear of the tent. Another cord connected to a foot pedal that lay obscured by the rug. This, B felt sure, was how Le Fay operated the cauldron.

She peeked inside the cauldron and saw a coiled-up mess of plastic tubing, with ends attached to the inner lip of the pot. Looking closer, she saw one tube labeled FOAM and the other, SMOKE. A plastic lid fit over the top, making it look like a boiling kettle of green goo. It was easy to see how this top, vibrating a bit, with bubbles spilling over the side, would look from a distance like a witch's cauldron from a scary Halloween movie.

"Holy cats," B murmured.

Just then, B heard voices approaching. She ducked behind the cauldron. It was Enchantress Le Fay, talking to . . . *Jason*! Jason Jameson. And they were approaching the tent.

B looked around. Was there a back way out? She couldn't tell in the dim light. There was a footstep at the back of the stage.

B went the only place she could go. Face-first, into the cauldron.

Chapter 10

She pulled her legs in just as a beam of light entered the tent. Someone had opened the curtain. She was twisted uncomfortably, with cauldron tubing pressed against her face. Enchantress Le Fay and Jason were coming! What if they looked into the cauldron?

"C-A-M-O-U-F-L-A-G-E," she whispered, hoping it wouldn't turn her shades of khaki and green like George's favorite pants.

"I promise I won't be late, Enchantress Le Fay," Jason was saying. "I'll be here right after school tomorrow."

"Call me 'Your Greatness,'" the fake witch replied. "We don't need all this 'Enchantress' business here.

The show starts at six, but I need you here right after school. There's a lot to prepare, and I can't afford any mess-ups at tomorrow's show. The Grand Spectacular is where I always make my biggest haul."

There was a moment of silence. "Haul?" Jason finally asked.

"It means, Jimmy, that it's where I take in the most money."

"Oh." Jason paused. "Your Greatness?"

"Yeah?"

"My name's not Jimmy. It's Jason."

"Close enough. Listen up, we've got things to discuss." B listened closely as Le Fay explained where all the hidden cords and switches were that made the bats with battery-powered red eyes flap, crystal balls levitate, and the creepy sound effects play at just the right time.

"Next, the cauldron," Le Fay said. "Before the show starts, make sure it's plugged in, and test the pedal to make sure both hoses are working. Toe on the pedal makes smoke, heel on the pedal makes bubbles. When the curtain opens, you need to make lots of smoke. See?"

They tested the cauldron, and B had a moment of terror, wondering if she'd get an electric shock. But all she felt was the burbling of bubbles passing through the tubes. At one point, Enchantress Le Fay looked right into the cauldron, and B's heart nearly stopped. But she seemed satisfied with what she saw, and went back to coaching Jason, while B practically melted into a puddle of relief.

"When folks start wanting to buy potions, be sure you've got lots ready to pass out," she said. "Load up with little bottles, and work the crowd."

"How do I know which potion is which?" Jason asked. "How do I tell money from love from success and stuff?"

Enchantress Le Fay laughed. "Don't you get it? It doesn't matter! It's all the same stuff."

B could see Jason's face as he processed this revelation. "You mean . . . there's no magic at all?"

Enchantress Le Fay laughed again.

"I . . . I thought you said you were going to teach me magic!" Jason cried.

Enchantress Le Fay leaned over and looked Jason in the eye.

"Oh, I've got magic all right, kid," she said. "And I'll teach it to you. You watch me close. I'll show you how I get fools and idiots to give me their money, night after night. You get good enough at that, you'll be rich. That's magic, isn't it? Best kind of magic, if you ask me."

B's anger bubbled like fake cauldron foam. This greedy, selfish, ridiculous woman didn't even care if she made people's lives miserable, so long as she earned a quick buck. B thought of Madame Mel and the High Dictums: Never use your magic to harm others. You can't make something from nothing, and you should never use magic to try to get rich. Enchantress Le Fay didn't even have real magic, yet she'd torn the Three High Dictums into tiny pieces, and ruined George's week. She needed to be taught a lesson — but how?

"You go and round up an audience, while I

grab Frank to announce me," Enchantress Le Fay snapped at Jason. "The show will start in five minutes."

B realized this was her only chance to get out of there before she got caught.

She waited until it was quiet and then raised her head over the rim of the cauldron. Enchantress Le Fay and Jason Jameson were gone.

B crawled out of the cauldron, uncamouflaged herself, slipped through the tent flaps, and ran straight into Mr. Bishop.

"There you are, B," Mr. Bishop said.

"S-sorry," B stammered. "I . . ."

Mr. Bishop stroked his goatee. "You must be eager to see the show."

"Actually," B began, "I think I've got my answer. . . ."

But just then, the announcer in his wrinkled red tuxedo jacket shouted out, "Step right up, ladies and, um, gentle*man*, for a show you won't soon forget."

"Looks like today's lesson is about to begin," Mr. Bishop whispered.

B didn't want to stick around for the trickery, but since she'd begged Mr. Bishop to come, she didn't have any choice.

The announcer was still announcing. "From the far reaches of time, from the dark forests of Olde England, comes a living descendant of Morgan Le Fay, the sorceress who bedazzled King Arthur's court! Need a love potion? A cure for baldness?" He glanced at Mr. Bishop. "Or, in your case, too much hair? Searching for the elixir of life? Look no further! Enchantress Le Fay waits to help you!"

He pulled the curtain rope, and Enchantress Le Fay stepped out with a flourish. She looked around, expecting applause, but got none. After all, it was only Mr. Bishop and B in the audience today. B was relieved to see that Jason Jameson wasn't back yet.

Enchantress Le Fay sized up Mr. Bishop the way B's father looked at sports cars. "Come closer, come closer," she said, beckoning to them in her gravelly voice. "The mysterious gentleman and the charming young lady. What has brought you to Enchantress

Le Fay today? What hidden needs, what deep desires can I help you with?"

She winked at Mr. Bishop. B giggled. Enchantress Le Fay shot her an annoyed glance. In a completely different voice, she said, "Hey, weren't you here the other day? With that obnoxious kid?"

B bristled at this description of her best friend.

Enchantress Le Fay turned her attention back to Mr. Bishop, took a deep breath, and resumed her stage voice. "You, sir . . . the spirits are vague, I can't sense your name like I usually can. . . ."

"Doug," Mr. Bishop said.

"Doug! I was just about to say that. The spirits are vague, *yessssss*, but your aura tells me you have powers all your own. What can Enchantress Le Fay *dooooo* for you?"

Mr. Bishop glanced at B and rolled his eyes slightly. "My special power," he told the witch, "is teaching. I came today to teach my student a lesson in good judgment."

"Ah!" Enchantress Le Fay reached for her suitcase and searched through the potions. "A teacher! A wise man and his pupil. What you need is a potion for knowledge! Drink this, and the hidden mysteries of the universe will unfold before you! Only fifty dollars." She held out an amber vial.

Mr. Bishop's left eyebrow rose. He shook his head.

Enchantress Le Fay selected a red vial from the cluttered case, and leaned a little closer to him. "Then perhaps you'd be interested in my very own, never fail, Cupid's arrow love potion? Only twenty-five dollars. I can demonstrate how it works."

Mr. Bishop coughed. "Er, no, thanks."

Enchantress Le Fay deflated slightly. "Good luck for fifteen?" She watched both their faces. "Happiness for ten?" She snapped her fingers under their noses. "I know what you need. The ever-popular money potion, sure to bring financial success, special today, only five dollars a dose!" She thrust a green vial into Mr. Bishop's hand.

"Why would the money potion cost the least?" B asked.

"If somebody can only afford five bucks, that's probably what they need most, kid," Enchantress Le Fay said.

To B's surprise, Mr. Bishop pulled out his wallet and handed Enchantress Le Fay a five-dollar bill. "Teachers never make enough," he said, laughing a little to himself. "Well, Madam, thanks for an entertaining show." He turned to leave.

"But I've only just begun!" she cried. A puff of green smoke rose from her cauldron. "Stay and see the rest!"

"Not today, thanks," Mr. Bishop said. In a low voice, he told B, "We've seen plenty."

"Be sure to come back tomorrow night for my Grand Spectacular Extravaganza," Enchantress Le Fay called after them. "It's the highlight of the fair! The whole town will be there. . . ."

Her voice faded as Mr. Bishop led B to a bench some distance from the thoroughfare, where no one would hear them talking. He uncorked the vial of money potion and poured a few drops into his hand. He tilted his hand so B could see it in the afternoon light.

"Look like a magical potion to you, B?" he asked.

"No," B said. "Mine, at least, was sparkly. That looks like salad dressing, except it's green."

"Take a whiff," Mr. Bishop said. "It's safe."

She sniffed at the little puddle in Mr. Bishop's palm. "It smells like the herb soap my Granny Grogg makes."

"Exactly," Mr. Bishop said. "Some herbs, some vegetable oil, and wham, a so-called potion, just enough to swindle poor, hopeful people out of their hard-earned money." Mr. Bishop reached for a napkin from a hot dog cart passing by, and wiped the potion oil off his hand. "But I should hope that after meeting her, you wouldn't need me to tell you she's no witch. Think of your parents. Think of everyone you've met at the Magical Rhyming Society. Are they anything like Enchantress Le Fay?"

"No, of course not," B said, kicking the dirt. "It's just . . . George is so shaken up by this, and everything seems to be going wrong for him. I wanted to make sure."

Mr. Bishop nodded. "People can get ideas into their heads and start believing them for crazy reasons, just because someone says so. It's called the power of suggestion. That's how Enchantress Le Fay's potions operate."

"George didn't believe her, though," B protested. "That's the thing. He was saying right to her face that he thought it was ridiculous. That's why she cursed him in the first place. And then his go-cart broke, and I think he got spooked."

"That's exactly it," Mr. Bishop said. "Even though he didn't believe it, a little superstitious part of his mind said, 'What if it is true?'"

The smell of fried dough with powdered sugar made B's stomach rumble, but she couldn't stop worrying about her friend. She picked up the half-empty potion vial and let the rest of it dribble onto the hard-packed fairground dust. "What can I do for him, then?" she asked.

Mr. Bishop stood up. "He'll snap out of it. Believe me." He pulled a book out of his knapsack. It was bound with a metal spine and pink jeweled lettering, and looked like a cross between an ancient book of spells and a teenage magazine. *Preteen Potions*, it read. "It's time to go. But since you managed to talk me out of a regular magic lesson, you'll have homework tonight. Read chapter two and be ready to discuss potions to cure the common cold next time we meet."

B took the book. "Um, Mr. Bishop? What do I say if someone sees me reading *Preteen Potions* on the bus?"

"Oh, right." Mr. Bishop cleared his throat.

"Mumbly-jumble, magical book,
Make for yourself a nonmagical look."

And the potions book turned into the Yellow Pages.

"Gee, thanks," B said as Mr. Bishop walked away.

B realized now that "Enchantress" Le Fay couldn't even curse a jelly doughnut. But that didn't make her harmless. People shouldn't pretend to have powers, and they shouldn't go around trying to scare people. Especially not B's best friend.

Enchantress Le Fay, B decided, had tangled with the wrong witch.

Now all B needed was a plan.

Chapter 11

"Pass the bird, please."

B handed her dad the steaming platter that held a perfectly golden brown roast chicken flanked by potatoes and carrots. A masterpiece for most cooks, just a normal dinner at B's house. B's mother's cooking spells were legendary in the witching world.

B poured an extra dollop of gravy over her potatoes. "This is amazing, Mom."

"Thanks, dear. You don't think the meat's too dry?"

"Are you kidding?" B took a huge bite. "Scrumptious."

"Then why isn't your sister touching her food?"

All eyes at the dinner table turned to Dawn, who sat staring at the solitary carrot on her plate, her chin resting in one hand.

B was concerned. "What's the matter, Dawn?"

"It's my magic lessons," Dawn muttered. "I'm going to fail my advanced potions seminar, and then they'll probably give my slot at Summer Enchantments Camp to someone else." She buried her face in her hands.

B knew all about Summer Enchantments Camp for teenage witches. Dawn had only been talking about it nonstop since she turned fourteen. Teenage witches from several nearby states gathered at Camp Juju and communed with nature while practicing advanced magic under the full moon and whatnot. B never knew what Dawn was more excited about — the magic, or the "totally hot guys," as she always described them, especially Lancelot Jackson, the seventeen-year-old spell-casting superstar.

B's mom loaded Dawn's plate. "Eat, pumpkin," she said. "Everything looks worse on an empty stomach."

"I've got a stomachache," Dawn protested. "From testing my healing potion."

B's parents exchanged worried looks.

"And look at my face!" Dawn cried, parting her hands. "My beauty potion made me break out in *pimples*! I look like a pizza face!"

"No, you don't," her mother said, clucking her tongue.

"Now, why would a lovely girl like you even think of making a beauty potion?" Dad asked. "You can't improve perfection."

Dawn groaned. "It's no use trying to cheer me up. I'm doomed. If I don't turn in a working honesty potion in two days, that's it. Kaput. Failing marks, which means no camp."

Honesty potion. Now there was an interesting idea. "What are the ingredients in an honesty potion, Dawn?" B asked.

Dawn looked up as if the answer to her potion misery was somehow scrawled on the ceiling. "You need something to expand the mind, something to loosen the tongue, something to, um, infuse the soul with courage, and something to fill the heart with truth."

"Yikes!" B said. "That's not a recipe, that's a mystery."

"Right. And that's why I'll end up magically mopping floors the rest of my life."

"But, girls, that's the wonderful thing about potions," their mother said. "They're not rigid recipes. They're creative! We would make potions in a factory if it was simple."

B watched her sister closely. Sometimes Dawn could be a drama queen, but this time, B could tell she was really worried.

"You'll figure it out, Dawn," B said. "Everything you do turns out well."

Dawn blinked. She looked at B for a long moment, then speared a chunk of chicken with her fork. "Thanks, B."

"I know another potion you should make," B said. "A fake curse antidote."

"A what?" Mom said.

"A fake curse antidote," B said. "George and I were at the fair, and we stopped to see this crazy so-called witch, Enchantress Le Fay. She did her silly show, and George said out loud there was no such thing as witchcraft, so Enchantress Le Fay put a curse on him."

Dawn chuckled. "No such thing as witchcraft, all right."

B's mother lay down her fork. "Surely George doesn't believe the curse is real."

"That's the thing," B said. "He didn't at first, but then all these bad things kept happening to him, and now he's convinced he's cursed. He stayed home from school today because he thinks he's deathly ill with a cold."

"Poor George!" B's mom said.

"Ridiculous," Dad said. "That boy needs to snap out of it. I thought he had more sense."

"Now, Felix," Mom said. "Emotions are tricky. It sounds like this Le Fay creature makes her living preying on people's emotions."

"And selling them potions," B added. "Hey, it rhymes! Could one of you think up a spell to stop her from something-something emotions with her something-something potions?"

"You're on your own, B," Dad said. "Why don't you spell something?"

"I've tried, but nothing helps," B said.

"You'll figure it out, B," Mom said, rising from her chair. "And you'll make a brilliant honesty potion, Dawn. I have complete faith in both of you. But right now, I have complete faith you'll both help me with the dishes."

Chapter 12

When they had finished the dishes, B followed Dawn up to her room, explaining about George.

"He's bringing it upon himself!" B was saying. "He's so sure he's cursed, he's practically useless. Thinking about the curse constantly. So of course bad things keep happening to him."

"Expand the mind, loosen the tongue . . ." Dawn was muttering to herself. "Hm? Oh. Yeah, George. He's got it pretty bad, huh?"

"He's totally paranoid," B said. Nightshade leaped up onto Dawn's bed and Dawn sat down in front of her cauldron.

"Hm. Whaddya think of this, B? A dictionary to

expand the mind, a picture of a sunset to fill the heart with truth . . ."

"That's interesting. Why a sunset?" B asked.

"Well, nature is one of the truest things there is, don't you think? Nature can't lie."

B stroked Nightshade's fur. "I like that, Dawn. That's really clever."

Dawn looked surprised, but she smiled. "Thanks. Anyway, what would infuse the soul with courage?"

B scratched Nightshade between the ears. "Umm . . . I don't know. I'm the biggest scaredy-cat there is."

"No, you're not. Think what you did at the Magical Rhyming Society when you found your magic! You did amazing spells in front of everyone!"

B flushed with pleasure to hear her sister's praise. "Yeah, but you know what? I couldn't do it until you came and stood next to me. *You* gave me courage."

"Well, I only went up because you needed me. Otherwise I'd have been scared, too . . ." Dawn trailed off midsentence and stared at B. Then she snapped her fingers. "That's it, B. You figured it out. It's family that gives us courage, isn't it?" Dawn grabbed a copy of their family's photo Christmas card that was lying on her desk and dropped it into her shiny EZ-Brew cauldron.

"And friends," B said. She gestured to the cauldron, where the family photo was melting into potion broth. "I hope Mom has more of those pictures."

"Now all I need is something to loosen the tongue."

"Um, a drink of water? The principal always takes a drink before starting his 'Welcome back to school' speech."

Dawn frowned. "I don't think that's what they mean."

"How about a thumbtack?"

Dawn stirred her cauldron with a wooden spoon. "What are you talking about?"

"Well, if you sat on a thumbtack, you'd make some noise in a hurry."

"You're crazy."

"Laughter loosens the tongue," B said. "It gets people talking."

Dawn froze midstir. "B, you might be a genius," she said. "Can I raid your candy stash?"

"Since when do you ask? Go ahead," B said, "but there's nothing very good left."

Dawn disappeared into B's room and came back with the Easter basket B had had since she was tiny. She kept it supplied with candy year-round. Dawn fished through it, then held a little green-wrapped square high in the air. "Aha!" she said. "Laffy Taffy."

She threw it into the cauldron and stirred. "Wish me luck, little sister," she said, then closed her eyes and recited a spell.

"Wisdom of years, innocence of youth,
Distill in my cauldron the essence of truth!"

There was a soft noise like the ringing of far-away chimes, and the lumpy glop of Dawn's ingredients transformed into a smooth sea green sauce that smelled like buttered popcorn.

Dawn and B peered over the lid at the surface of the brew.

"Please, oh please, oh please," Dawn whispered. "Here goes nothing." She dipped the spoon in, then licked it clean.

"Tastes good," Dawn said. "Go ahead, quiz me."

"Okay," B said. "Did you or did you not fib to Mom and Dad two years ago about the broken crystal ball?"

Dawn's face flushed scarlet. "Yes!" She pressed her lips together. "It was a tiny white lie, okay? And I hadn't been using it. I was just *looking* at it."

"Right," B said. "What else do you do with a crystal ball, go bowling?"

"No, you tell the future with it," Dawn said. "Oh, for heaven's sake." Then her scowl turned into a radiant smile. "My potion worked! It made me tell the truth!"

"Not so fast," B said. "How much of your waking time do you spend daydreaming about Lancelot Jackson?"

Dawn whapped B lightly on the hand with her wooden spoon. "You little sneak!" She tried to clamp her lips together, but they had a mind of their own.

"Sixty-six percent." She clapped her hand over her mouth.

"The numbers don't lie, do they?" B said, grinning. "Looks like you'll get to go to Camp Juju. Congratulations."

Dawn sank down into her chair, exhausted and relieved. "It really works, doesn't it?"

"It's spectacular."

Spectacular. The Grand Spectacular! Holy cats. Nothing like a little honesty mixed into a bamboozler's performance . . . She snapped her fingers. That was it — the secret weapon she needed.

"Hey, Dawn, I promise not to ask you any more personal questions if you let me take some of this potion. I think I want it for Enchantress Le Fay's Grand Spectacular tomorrow."

Dawn cocked an eyebrow. "What're you cooking up, little sis?"

"Nothing much. Just a fake curse antidote."

"Be careful," Dawn said. "With honesty, you can get more than you bargained for."

B went to her room, picked up the phone, and dialed.

The voice on the other line sounded near death. "H'lo."

"George?"

"This isn't George. It's his cursed twin," her friend said gloomily.

"Pull-leeeze," B said. "Listen, George, I've got a guaranteed way to break Enchantress Le Fay's curse."

George didn't say anything.

"If I promise to get rid of the curse, forever, will you do what I ask you to, even if you don't like it?"

"Why do I have a bad feeling about this?" George moaned.

"You've got a bad feeling about everything lately," B said. "Trust me. I'm your best friend. Would I do something to hurt you?"

"Not on purpose," George said.

"Do you *promise*?"

George sighed. "If it's legal."

"'Course it's legal! And it's easy. All you've got to do is come to the fair tomorrow to see the Grand Spectacular."

Chapter 13

The next day, B waited for George on the steps of the school. The late bus came and went, but still no George. B was just about to go in when she saw a figure running up the long driveway to the school. Tall, with a crazy shag of blond curls, running as fast as a soccer star . . . yep, it was George.

"What are you doing?" B called to him. "How come you weren't on the bus?"

"Missed it," he panted, catching up to her. "Lost homework. Spilled oatmeal. Forgot to walk Butterbrains."

B wrinkled her nose. *"Pee-yew!* What's that smell?"

George lifted up one of his huge sneakers. "Oh, *no*."

There, smashed into the bottom of his soccer shoe, was a big brown clump of . . .

"Gross!" George wailed, scuffing his foot furiously into the grass. "I'm gonna smell like dog doo all day! I am *so* completely cursed!"

B dragged George by the backpack up the steps of the school. "Knock it off! You're *not* cursed. It's just another bad morning. Come on. Er" — she wrinkled her nose once more — "you might want to walk on your tippy-toes till we get this cleaned up."

They got the shoe cleaned, but George's day didn't improve much. B watched as her friend walked around all day in a daze, bumping into things, calling teachers by the wrong names, and fidgeting nervously instead of listening during class. At lunchtime he announced he'd better quit the soccer team, so his curse couldn't make them lose their chance at the league play-offs. B shadowed him all during gym class so she could tackle him in case he tried to tell Coach Lyons he was quitting.

By the end of the day, she was exhausted. Babysitting a curse, she decided, was no fun.

"Look," B said. "This will all be over tonight. See you at the Grand Spectacular, at six o'clock."

George looked doubtful.

"You promise you'll come?" B demanded.

"Okay," George said. "If I can get there in one piece."

At five-fifteen B pulled on her jacket and stepped outside to get to the fair early. It was a perfect fall evening — a chill breeze swept the scent of leaves into the air, and a burning orange sunset painted the sky to the west. B patted her pocket containing the potion vial that Mr. Bishop had bought at the fair, now full to the cork with a dose of Dawn's honesty potion.

She smiled to herself. Le Fay's shenanigans would crumple as soon as Dawn's honesty potion got inside her. The tricky part would be getting her to drink it. It wouldn't be easy. But for George, B would find a way.

The sky had turned purple by the time B reached the park, and the fair lights flashed wildly. B hurried through the noisy Friday night crowd to the tent that became Enchantress Le Fay's little stage once the curtain opened. A large poster, crookedly hung on the tent, announced tonight's Grand Spectacular, but no spectators had lined up yet. B ducked under a canvas flap.

There was no one inside the tent, which doubled as "backstage." She checked her watch. 5:40. The show started at six o'clock, and no Le Fay or Jason! Outside the tent, B knew, the crowd would start gathering soon. B ducked behind a side curtain.

Her eyes had just adjusted to the dark when footsteps on the platform behind her made B turn around. It was Enchantress Le Fay, dressed in a different black dress — still raggedy, but with sequins — holding her wig and her makeup bag. "Jimmy!" she called. "I need you to go back to my camper and get my set of shrunken heads. The rubber ones . . . Oh!" She stopped in her tracks; the torn strips of fabric that made up her skirt were rustling. "You're that girl who was with the bratty boy, and then with the teacher guy."

"Yep," B said. "That's me. I, uh, go to school with Jason, your helper."

"Really? That's nice." She sat down at a little table, flicked on a portable light, and started painting thick makeup on her face. "Where did he go? And what are you doing here?"

"I'm here to help," B said. "Jason is, uh, running late."

Le Fay swiveled around on her bench. "Figures! I don't know why I bother with that kid. I need him here in just" — she checked her watch — "a few minutes. He's got to help me before the show."

"Well, since he's not here," B said, "why not use me? I've heard, I mean, I know about the tricks you use to help make your show spooky."

Enchantress Le Fay applied her thick dark eyeliner while she talked to B. "Name one."

B flipped the switch for the bats, and lowered the lever that made a crystal ball (glass, fake) seem to levitate. She even tested the music.

"Hm," Le Fay said. "I guess you do know the drill. Okay, you can stay. Fasten my necklace, will you?" While B fumbled with the tiny clasp of one of her brass charms, Le Fay lined her lips with a red pencil, then smeared on a thick coat of scarlet lipstick. When she was done, she made a kissing noise at her reflection in a handheld mirror. *"Mmm-wah!"* B had to work hard not to laugh.

B checked her watch again. 5:45. Now was her moment. For her plan to work, B needed Enchantress Le Fay to lose sight of what time it was, so she wouldn't rush to get ready for the show. B stared at the fake witch's watch, and breathed, "S-T-O-P." The second hand stopped spinning.

"Like my Grand Spectacular dress?" Le Fay said. "I'm adding a favorite trick of mine tonight. You can help me set it up. Open that box over in the corner and get out the witch hat inside. Then open the cage under the hat, but be careful, because Rufus the rabbit's in there. Don't worry, he won't bite. Just slip him in the secret pouch in the hat. I'll start with that trick — the audiences always love it."

B followed the instructions, giving Rufus a quick scratch behind his ears. Sweet little bunny, too bad he had to put up with stuff like this. She tucked him carefully into the compartment inside the sequin-covered hat.

Le Fay was apparently in a talkative mood. "Man, oh, man, am I in trouble tonight," she said, plastering her face with dark rouge. "Running late for the show! We'll just have to skip the shrunken heads. My assistant, gone. How's a poor gal gonna earn a buck?"

"Are you sure you're running late?" B said. "What time is it?"

"Well, whaddya know," Le Fay said, glancing again at her watch. "I've still got a little wiggle room. Here, stick a few of these glow-in-the-dark spiders into my wig."

B arranged the spiders, then reached into her pocket and pulled out Dawn's honesty potion. She was so close! Maybe George was on the other side of the curtain right now, waiting for the show to start. B desperately hoped so — him and half the town, too, with any good luck. But if Enchantress

Le Fay didn't somehow drink this potion, what good would it do? If she wasn't forced to admit the truth, how could B prove to George that the curse was bogus?

"Is your throat sore?" B asked. "I could get you a drink of water." B didn't wait for an answer. She headed for the exit to find a drink. In the dim light she tripped, knocking over the suitcase full of vials. Dawn's honesty potion vial spun out of her fingers and landed in the middle of dozens of others.

And there was no way to tell them apart.

Chapter 14

"Nice going, klutzy," Enchantress Le Fay snarled. "Clean those up!"

"Sorry about that," B said, trying to keep her voice calm while she scooped up potion bottles, dumped them helter-skelter in the suitcase, and desperately searched for one that looked different.

But nothing looked different. B started uncorking bottles and sniffing them. They all had that mild herbal scent that Mr. Bishop's money potion had had. B hoped Enchantress Le Fay wouldn't notice her sniffing each one.

No such luck.

"What are you doing with the potions?" Le Fay cried.

"Oh!" B stalled to think of something. "I, um, thought I'd label them."

Enchantress Le Fay started pinning her blond hair off her face with bobby pins. "Nice idea," she said. "But I don't think there's time for that."

Sniff. "Oh, I'm pretty quick." *Sniff.* "They all sort of smell the same, don't they?" *Sniff.*

"That's because they *are* the same."

Sniff. "Right."

B checked her watch again. 5:58! Almost showtime . . . but where was that honesty potion?

"Listen to that crowd gathering out there," Enchantress Le Fay bragged. "I'll make a fortune tonight. Sounds like hundreds! Lining up fifteen minutes early, just to see me. You don't see that kind of showbiz success every day, you know."

"I'm sure you don't," B agreed. She got up and peeked her head through the curtain. George had come! She yanked her head back in before he turned and saw her. "It sure is a big crowd, Miss Le Fay." *The bigger, the better!* She returned to the spilled potions, searching through them as quickly as she could.

But each bottle was the same. About to give up, B uncorked one more bottle and took a deep whiff.

This bottle was different. It smelled like buttered popcorn. The honesty potion! Just in time. B had breathed it in so deeply, her nostrils tickled. Come to think of it, her head felt light and fluttery for a moment.

Oh, no!

She sniffed one more time. Sure enough, the fragrance was gone.

She'd found the genuine potion among the fakes . . . and used up all its magic potency!

How could she trick Le Fay into telling the truth now? Come to think of it, how could she trick anyone when she, herself, was forced to only speak the truth?

Her whole plan was ruined!

Footsteps clattered up the back steps. "Sorry I'm late, Your Greatness!" Jason Jameson cried, bursting through the curtain, dressed in a ridiculous wizard's costume — a bathrobe decorated with puffy paint stars. "My mom made me wash all the dish —

hey!" He pointed at B. "What're you doing here, Beeswax?"

B scowled at Jason, but the honesty spell had ideas of its own. "I'm here to expose Enchantress Le Fay for the flashy fraud she really is," she said.

For a second Jason, Le Fay, and B were frozen, no one knowing how to react.

Then Enchantress Le Fay's throaty laugh reverberated through the tent. "I like your attitude," she said. "'Flashy fraud!' Think you can take me down, do you? Ha! You've got guts, Miss Beeswax. Too bad you don't like me. I could really use an apprentice like you."

"Hey!" Jason said. "What about me?"

Le Fay shrugged and kept fussing with her props.

B backed away, bumping into the cauldron. She wished she could hop back inside it and camouflage herself again, she was so embarrassed and disappointed. There on the other side of that curtain was George, hoping and waiting for B to break the curse. And she'd blown her chance.

Jason sneered at B. "It'll take more than a stink-bug like you to mess up Enchantress Le Fay's show," he said. "She's a *professional* witch. An *expert*."

"Listen here, sugar pie," Enchantress Le Fay said, fastening a plastic wart to her cheek. "Not even a real witch could stop me from making a killing tonight. Stick around, you may learn something."

Wait a minute.

A real witch. A professional. An expert.

B checked the time once more. Six o'clock.

Showtime.

It was now or never, even if Dawn's honesty potion had gone up the wrong nose. Time to show George, and the whole town, what a so-called enchantress's curses were worth.

Of course! she thought. *I still have my magic. There must be something I can do.*

The announcer poked his handlebar mustache through the curtain. "It's time to roll. Got a full house tonight."

Le Fay looked at her watch. "Eeeek!" she cried, shaking her wrist. "Lousy batteries! This says I've got fifteen more minutes."

The announcer shook his head. "Six-oh-two right now."

Jason and Le Fay began racing around like bumper cars, colliding in their haste to get ready.

"Well," B said nonchalantly, "since there's no way I can outwit a professional, expert witch, I guess I'll just go out in the audience and watch the show."

Jason and Le Fay were too frantic to answer.

"Good luck," B said. Under her breath she added, "You're going to need it."

Chapter 15

B slipped down the back steps and circled around to join George in front of the curtain. They were in the front row.

"Well, I'm here," he said. "What've you got up your sleeve?"

"A few magic tricks of my own," B said. The honesty potion was still in effect but she hoped George wouldn't realize that she was telling the truth.

George looked even more worried now, to be facing Enchantress Le Fay.

B tried to look confident. "Don't worry," she said. "You'll get cured tonight, one way or another."

"I hope so. On the way here, I stopped to cross the street, and the traffic light broke. It never turned red so that I could cross. The cars were backed up for miles." George folded his arms across his chest. "I'm a walking curse."

B swallowed and nodded toward the opening curtain. "Watch and see what happens."

The curtain parted just enough for the announcer to step forward. "Hear ye, hear ye, ladies and gentlemen," he said. "From the far reaches of time, from the dark forests of Olde England, comes a sorceress whose amazing powers you've witnessed this entire week that the fair has been in town. But nothing, my friends, I tell you, nothing has prepared you for the dazzling feats of magical skill, the amazing miracles of healing you're about to see tonight! Behold, I give you Enchantress Le Fay and her Grand Spectacular!"

The audience thundered its applause as the curtain opened the rest of the way, revealing a sparkling Enchantress Le Fay, the spotlights illuminating her fancy dress and hat.

Jason gestured toward her over and over, like a game show hostess pointing to the fabulous prizes. Le Fay took a deep curtsey, then pressed both her palms together.

"Good *eve*ning, my friends," she purred. She opened her arms wide, her fingers outstretched as if she was ready to give the audience a huge, witchy hug. "I can *feel* the *needs* and *desires*, the *aches* and *pains* of everyone here tonight! They press upon me with a terrible weight." She thrust both arms high in the air. "But I shall *lift* them off your shoulders with my mystic potions! And after this night, you will suffer no more."

B elbowed George. "Told ya. After tonight, you'll suffer no more."

"*Hsh!*" George hissed. "Don't draw her attention to me!"

Too late. Enchantress Le Fay caught sight of George standing next to B, and frowned. "But since there are some here who may still doubt my power, I'll begin with a demonstration."

She whipped off her tall, sequined hat, and held

it so the audience could see the inside. "Behold, my hat! Empty, is it not?"

Everyone except B agreed that it looked empty.

She held it straight upside down. "Apprentice," she barked to Jason, "my wand."

Jason handed her a black wand with a white tip. She waved it in slow circles over the hat. *"Nebbity nobbledy hippity hop!"* She tapped the hat, then reached in and pulled out poor Rufus by the scruff of the neck. She held him high in the air, triumphant.

The audience clapped wildly. Under the cover of their noise, B filled her mind with thoughts of Rufus, and spelled, "M-U-L-T-I-P-L-Y."

A pair of white ears poked up out of the hat. Then another, and another. One by one, rabbits began hopping out of the hat. B thought she saw pieces of lint being transformed into new rabbits — but she hoped it would stop soon, because she wasn't sure, and she didn't want to turn anything else into a bunny! The crowd *ooh*ed and *aah*ed, but the fake witch looked horrified.

"Oh!" Le Fay cried, and, "Ack! Catch them, apprentice!"

Jason scrambled for bunnies while dozens more rabbits poured over the hat brim, cascading out like popcorn overflowing a hot air popper. Jason couldn't catch a single one.

Le Fay looked desperately this way and that, still clutching Rufus by the nape of his neck. The poor little guy looked miserable, his paws dangling in midair.

B smiled to herself. Maybe Rufus the rabbit had a story to tell.

"S-P-E-A-K," she whispered.

Since B and George were in the front row, B could just make out what the rabbit was saying. "Hey, Laaaaa-dy," Rufus whined, "are you planning on putting me down any time soon?" He kicked out a long hind paw, which made him spin like a piñata.

Enchantress Le Fay's eyeballs bulged. She nearly dropped Rufus. Le Fay gulped and tried to smile, clearly baffled at this new development.

"I . . . uh . . ." Enchantress Le Fay was trying to regain control and keep the show going.

"She doesn't look okay," George whispered.

B giggled. "I think she's having an attack of conscience about her bunnies."

"I'm serious," Rufus said, kicking his legs in midair once more. "How would you like it, strung up here like a side of bacon while someone holds you by the hair?"

Slowly, Le Fay held Rufus as far from her face as she could, as if she was afraid he might bite her. "Behold!" she said shakily. "My powers have conjured up a talking rabbit!"

Someone in the audience snickered.

"Do not doubt me! I have just heard him speak with my own ears!" she screeched. Then she poked the rabbit with her wand. "Say something!"

"S-P-E-E-C-H-L-E-S-S," B murmured, her lips barely moving.

Le Fay waited and the crowd grew restless.

B thought she saw beads of sweat dripping down her makeup-plastered face. Desperate, Le Fay tried to say something out of the corner of her own mouth. "Enchantress Le Fay is amazing!"

"Boo!" shouted a pair of teenagers in the back. "That's not the rabbit talking!"

Enchantress Le Fay picked up her hat, stuffed Rufus back inside, and wedged it firmly on her head. "Moving on," she said briskly, "let me summon my floating crystal ball to tell your fortunes. Is there someone in the audience who needs to know what their future holds?"

Float. Now there was an interesting idea.

B stared at the hat and spelled the word.

Enchantress Le Fay's sequined hat rose off her head. And so did her wig! Together, they floated across the stage.

Enchantress Le Fay shrieked. Wisps of blond hair escaped from their pins and stuck out in every direction. "Grab it, Jimmy!" she cried.

Rufus poked his head out from under the brim of the hat. B gasped. The rabbit had escaped his secret pouch, and gotten his paws tangled up in Le Fay's wig! B giggled. Brilliant! Now, why hadn't she thought of that?

Enchantress Le Fay tried to grab at her floating wig while the audience thundered with laughter.

"That's not part of the show!" she shouted. "I'm not doing that."

Jason looked up at the floating wig in horror. "Then it must be real magic," he said.

"Get the phony witch off the stage!" someone else cried out.

Enchantress Le Fay clenched her fists and shook them in the air. A whining squeal boiled up inside her, seemingly from the tips of her toes. "Oooooh, this cannot be happening!" she cried, stamping her foot, and forgetting completely to use her Enchantress voice. "There is *no such thing* as magic!"

For a moment, everyone was still.

Enchantress Le Fay clapped a hand over her mouth, turned, and ran off the stage.

B caught sight of George's face, his mouth dropped open. She hoped this would be enough to convince him.

Jason Jameson found himself alone on the stage. He pulled his wizard bathrobe a little tighter around himself.

B smiled inwardly, but her job wasn't over yet. She kept her eyes fixed on the floating hat. "L-A-N-D," she breathed, watching carefully as the hat gently floated to the floor.

The audience laughed. Sometimes finding out how the trick is done is as much fun as being tricked in the first place. B smiled. If only they *really* knew.

People began drifting away. Gradually, B relaxed. And Jason hurriedly began to close the curtain.

The bewildered-looking announcer appeared, urging everyone to visit the other attractions at the fair that night. In the moment when all other eyes were on his bobbing handlebar mustache, B saw a little white rabbit hop across the stage and slip out of the tent.

Chapter 16

The crowd dwindled quickly. Without a word, B and George walked away from Enchantress Le Fay's stage. Neither one of them looked back.

George kicked at a broken soda cup on the ground.

"So," B said eventually, "want to hit the roller coaster?"

An organ grinder and his monkey passed by. The monkey jumped up onto George's shoulder and tried to steal his glasses.

"Hey! Get off!"

The monkey leaped down, chattering his displeasure. B laughed, and finally, George did, too.

"I think I've had enough of the fair for one week," George said. "Let's go."

Soon the noise and lights were behind them. Crickets drowned out the carousel in no time.

"That was . . . strange," George said at length. "The bit with the rabbit was really convincing. I don't get why she fell apart and ran off, though, just because of her wig."

B scratched her chin thoughtfully. "She seemed pretty unstable, don't you think?"

George gave her a sharp look. "Did you have something to do with that?"

"What, I made her unstable?" B said, waving indignantly, grateful that the honesty potion had worn off. "How could I have had anything to do with it?"

"Hm." George nudged her with his elbow. "You made me come tonight, though. If I didn't know better, I'd think you had some kind of magic powers."

B laughed out loud — possibly, she thought, a little too loud. "So are you really cured?" she asked. "No more curse?"

George nodded. "No more curse. She was *not* a real witch."

B laughed. It felt so good to have George back — the real George, not the cursed zombie he'd been these last few days. Soon the fair would leave town, and all this trouble would be gone for good.

"I'm sorry I was such a pain," George said.

Good old George! B's spirits soared. She'd done it! She'd squashed George's curse and gotten her best friend back, and given Enchantress Le Fay a well-deserved lesson about real witchcraft while she was at it.

"Dad and I decided to take our tap dancing lessons right here in town," George said. "I figured, why try to hide it? There's nothing wrong with tap dancing."

"Exactly!" B said. "That's great. I'm glad to hear it."

"I don't know what was the matter with me," George said. "I know there are no witches. Knew it all along. I mean, how could there be?"

This time B's laugh was harder to manage. "Yeah, really," she said. "How could there be?"

They were nearly home. B's front porch lights twinkled invitingly, and Nightshade's silhouette waited on the top step.

They were just passing the Peabodys' driveway when a truck whizzed by, plowing straight through a huge mud puddle by the edge of the road.

An arc of spray rose in the air. B saw George about to get soaked. . . . More bad luck! No!

"S-T-O-P!" she cried.

The drops of water froze, suspended in midair, like they'd been captured in a photograph, while the truck taillights dwindled into pinpoints in the distance.

George looked at B, his mouth hanging open.

"What," he gulped, "was *that*?"

Oh, no.

Oh, no, no, no.

So much for secrets!

B's charmed adventures continue in

Read on for a sneak peek!

"Let me get this straight, B," George said, bouncing his soccer ball on his forehead. "All you have to do is spell a word, just some old random word, and you can make *anything* happen?"

Beatrix, "B" to her friends, flopped into the beanbag chair on her best friend's basement rec room floor. "It's not that simple, George," she said. "Watch out! You nearly hit the lamp."

George caught the ball. His thick, curly blond hair dangled over the rim of his glasses, but B could see the curiosity sparkling in his eyes. "W-I-N-D," she spelled, and a little breeze swept through the room, riffling her friend's hair.

George touched his forehead in amazement. "You really did that, didn't you? I still can't believe it." He began pacing back and forth. "So," he said, waving his hands wildly, "*so*, you could just spell 'win' and *bam*, our team could win the championship soccer game on Thursday? Just like that?" He wiggled his fingers.

B laughed. "No, I couldn't. And I wouldn't do a thing like that, even if I could."

Clearly, George didn't understand magic yet.

And why should he? It was all so new to him. She hadn't meant to tell him she was a witch — he found out by accident. All the same, it was a relief not to have to keep the secret from him anymore, and to have someone to talk to about her magic. She tried to explain herself better.

"Just because it's magic, George, doesn't mean it's like the movies. Real magic takes training, and lots of practice. There are rules! Even still, things have a way of going wrong." She held up her hands, and George tossed her the ball. "Believe me, I know."

She tried bouncing the ball on her forehead, but it got away from her and rolled across the broad room. George's huge yellow dog, Butterbrains, bounded after it.

"Show me another trick," George begged. "C'mon. One teensy little trick."

"They're not *tricks*," B said indignantly. "I'm not some circus performer. This is real."

"I know. Just one little . . . demonstration?"

"*Allllll* right," she said. "What do you want to see?"

George pointed at a lava lamp. "Make it, I dunno, float in the air or something." He fidgeted with excitement.

B focused on the lamp. "F-L-O-A-T," she said.

The lamp rose in the air and swung in a wide circle, as far as the power cord would let it travel. Butterbrains backed into a corner, his head cocked to one side. Now and then he gave a curious whimper, his tail thumping.

George crawled over to Butterbrains and tussled with him. "It's okay, boy! It's only B, the magic witch." He giggled. "This is just so stinking cool! I can't believe it. I can't *believe* it!"

B smiled. When George was excited about something, he had a one-track mind. How long, B wondered, would it take him to get used to her magic? She'd had a lifetime, growing up with parents and an older sister who were witches. True, their spells, like most other witches', were conjured by imaginative rhyming couplets, and not by spelling. Even so, minor magic such as floating objects had been commonplace in B's home for as long as she could remember.

Why not give him a little crash course?

"F-L-O-A-T," she whispered, concentrating on a plastic tote full of Wiffle balls and squooshy footballs. They slipped into the air silently and orbited over George's head.

"Whoa!" George paused in his game with Butterbrains. "Lookit that!"

Butterbrains barked and jumped in the air, his body twisting as he tried in vain to snag the flying balls.

"D-A-N-C-E," B told a tub full of old, forgotten action figures George had long since outgrown. Soon military figures were waltzing with monsters, and Greek heroes were tangoing with robots.

If George hung his mouth open any wider, he'd start drooling.

This was too much fun.

"B-U-I-L-D," she told a huge crate of interlocking blocks, and, clickety-clack, they flew out by the dozens to form themselves into a rainbow-colored replica of George's house, right down to the shrubs.

And still the lava lamp swung its wide arc, illuminating the bizarre party like a strobe light, while Butterbrains barked like a maniac.

"Oh, man," George said. "Think what you could do with this — the stuff you could pull off at school!" He doubled over laughing. "Just imagine, a school assembly, and you make the vice principal's toupee float all over the auditorium. *Attack of the bad hair monster!*"

B giggled. "No way! That's so mean. Besides, my magic is an absolute secret, remember? *No one* can find out about it."

"I know, I know," George said, still laughing. "You've gotta admit, though, that would be an assembly to remember." He pantomimed clutching at his head, as if his own hair had just flown away.

"Yeah, but you make me nervous, the way you keep bringing up ideas like that," B said, watching as the clackety building blocks turned George's house into a castle. "I would get in such huge trouble if the Magical Rhyming Society found out that you know about this."

George sat up, blinking at B. "There's a Magical Rhyming *Society*? You mean, there's lots of witches, all organized and stuff?"

"Yup. Lots of them." B aimed a G-L-O-W spell at a pair of glow-in-the-dark plastic swords. They began dueling each other in midair. "What, did you think I'm the only one?"

Butterbrains ran in frenetic circles, barking at the bobbling balls, the dancing figures, clashing swords, and building Legos, each in turn.

George shrugged. "How would I know? You're the only witch I've ever . . ."

KNOCK.

They stared at each other, terrified.

KNOCK.

Then they stared at the whirlwind of toys.

George's dad's voice came through the thin door. "What are you two doing to that dog?"

Meet the Kreeps

Check out the whole spooky series!

#1: There Goes the Neighborhood

#2: The New Step-Mummy

#3: The Nanny Nightmare

#4: The Mad Scientist

#5: Three's a Krowd

Tails of enchantment!

Read about a very special pet shop—
one where all the animals are magic!